Gator Kill

Bill Crider

Walker and Company
New York

First published in the United States of America in 1992 by Walker Publishing Company, Inc.

Published simultaneously in Canada by Thomas Allen & Son Canada, Limited, Markham, Ontario

Library of Congress Cataloging-in-Publication Data
Crider, Bill, 1941–
Gator kill / Bill Crider.
p.   cm.
ISBN 0-8027-3213-5
I. Title.
PS3553.R497G38   1992
813'.54—dc20   91-42478
CIP

Printed in the United States of America
2 4 6 8 10 9 7 5 3 1

To Barbara Puechner
agent and friend (what a great combination!)

▽

1

SOME PEOPLE SAY it's quiet and peaceful in the country at night. I guess they haven't been to the part of the country I was in.

Which is where?

About an hour or so west of Houston, in the river bottoms and marshy land around Eagle Lake. In that area, anyhow.

It was a hot, sticky September night, and my shirt was hanging on me like it had been doused with a bucket of water. I'd already sweated off most of the insect repellent I'd covered myself with earlier, and mosquitoes were singing all around me. I was tired of slapping at them, so quite a few were making a meal out of my tired old blood.

There were plenty of other noises besides the mosquitoes: about a million or so other kinds of insects, frogs, night birds, the wind in the cattails, an old bass hitting the top of the water, and now and then the bellow of a bull alligator.

"You ready to go?" Fred Benton asked me.

I gave him the standard Texas answer. "As ready as I'll ever be."

"Give 'er a shove, then," he said, and we slid the flat-bottomed aluminum johnboat off the bank and through some lily pads that brushed softly against its bottom and sides.

I jumped in without getting my running shoes completely soaked, but Fred didn't seem to mind the water. He stayed by the side of the boat until he was out calf-deep, then threw one dripping leg over the side and climbed in. Then he stood in the front of the boat and poled us along with a ten-foot stick he'd cut himself from an oak limb.

It was a dark night, the moon hidden in thick clouds that hardly seemed to move in the light south breeze.

"Ought to be plenty of 'em out here," Fred said. "Turn on your flashlight."

I had a new black plastic flashlight with a halogen bulb, and I thumbed the big white knob forward. The beam leapt across the water, picking up the water plants and cattails, throwing shadows behind them. The water almost seemed to boil with life, its surface rippled by fish, minnows, bugs, and whatever larger things lurked beneath it.

It wasn't long before the light picked up the red and shining eyes of a gator, and then more and more of them. They were what Fred had brought me to see.

I didn't know what it was about seeing alligators like that, floating along in complete silence, their eyes and nostrils just above the water's surface, that affected me so, but it did. I got a distinct chill that had not a thing in the world to do with the way the soft night breeze was blowing against my wet shirt. Goose bumps lined my arms.

"Those are just the little ones," Fred said.

Fred was a guy who would know, having owned the lake we were on for a long time, thirty or more years, and he'd always been one to like alligators. He once told me that he felt like he knew them personally.

He was a big man, six three or so, and still very solid despite the fact that his stomach had a tendency to hang over his belt these days. His hair was still mostly black, with just a few strands of gray sprinkled around, belying his age, which had to be near seventy.

"I'm gonna catch one for you," he said.

I wanted to tell him not to go to any trouble on my account, but he'd already laid his pole down in the boat and crouched near the side. When we drifted close enough to one he wanted, he reached in the water and came up with it.

"You gotta hold 'em just right," he said. He had one hand behind the gator's head and one on its tail. "They got more strength in these tails than you'd think. You let a big one get to swinging that tail, and it's good night, nurse. Here. Take him."

He stuck the gator out at me, and there was nothing to do but put down the flashlight and take him. Either that, or look like a sissy. Put one hundred men from Texas in that boat with Fred, and ninety-nine of them would take the alligator rather than risk looking bad. Men may talk about being more sensitive these days, more "in touch with their feelings," but the old macho games still matter to most of us. They still matter a lot.

Taking the gator wasn't so bad, since all I had to do was put my hands on the side of it opposite Fred's. He already had the grip. All I had to do was copy it.

"Folks are always surprised," Fred said.

I don't know how he knew I was surprised. He couldn't see my face. The moon was still concealed behind the clouds, and the flashlight was in the bottom of the boat.

But he was right. I was surprised.

"They always think that scaly old thing is gonna feel as rough as a cob," he said. "But it don't."

And it didn't. The gator's skin was surprisingly soft and smooth. Maybe that's why they made such good shoes out of them.

"How—" My voice cracked a little. The goose bumps on my arms were probably sticking up like pencil erasers by now. I started over. "How big is this one?"

Fred chuckled. "It's just a baby. Prob'ly not even two feet."

"Uh . . . you want him back?"

"Tell you what. I'll let you put him in the water."

There he went again, doing me favors I hadn't asked for.
"Uh—" I said.

"It's easy. Just don't get in a rush."

Not much chance of that, I thought. In my hands the gator strained against me.

"Just ease him down," Fred said. "Soon's you get him in the water, let go real quick."

Could I say, What if his mother comes by and bites my hand off? Of course I couldn't. That would make me look bad.

So I lowered the gator over the side, and almost at the instant he touched the water I let go. There was a slight splash and he was gone. The moon, slipping out from the clouds for a moment, reflected off the ripples.

Fred reached in the pocket of his old blue cotton work shirt and dug out a crumpled package of Camels. The ones without filters. He was the only person I knew who still smoked those things. Then he came up with a kitchen match, which he popped into flame with his thumbnail, a stunt I had always admired.

When he lit the cigarette, he said, "I just wanted you to see this." The coal of the cigarette moved as he waved his hand to indicate the area around us.

"It's been an education," I said.

"I thought it might be. You city boys don't get to see things like this just any old time."

"Hardly ever," I said. I reached over and got the flashlight, turned it off.

"So what do you think?"

"It's a great place. Especially if you like alligators."

"Well, I like 'em. How about you?"

"Maybe they grow on you," I said.

He shrugged. The boat rocked gently. "I wouldn't know about that. I think I've always liked 'em."

He smoked for a minute in silence. I sat there and listened to all the sounds of the night.

"Those old Spanish explorers didn't know what to make of 'em when they came over to this country," he said finally.

"Called 'em *el lagarto*. Means 'the lizard.' They look like lizards to you?"

"Not exactly," I said.

"Me either. But I guess it's as good a name as any."

He smoked some more. "Your daddy used to like 'em. Brought you out here to see 'em when you were just a kid."

I vaguely remembered the trip. We were living in Galveston, and my father had gone hunting somewhere near Eagle Lake on some land owned by Fred Benton. Goose hunting. Eagle Lake is the Goose Hunting Capital of the World, according to its boosters. Fred and my father had become friends. Later, one summer, he had taken me and my sister to see the alligators.

"Not here, though," I said.

"Naw, not here. I don't guess I'd bring a little kid out here. Too much excitement. Might fall in and let a gator eat him. Took you to one of the smaller lakes."

Fred's land was covered with lakes, some of them man-made, some of them natural. The natural ones had been there a long time. "Forever," is the way Fred put it.

My sister and I had seen some big gators, looking like black logs in the water. One of them had pushed himself up on the land and was lying across the trail where we were walking. That was the one I remembered best.

To me, he had looked as big as a railroad car lying there, the black skin dry from the hot air, the knobby back looking as impenetrable as armor plate.

He didn't move at all, not even to open his eyes, though he must have known that we were there.

We stood and looked at him for a while, then turned and went back another way. No one, not even the adults, wanted to try walking around him and risk passing within reach of that toothy mouth or that thick tail.

I asked Fred if he remembered it.

"Sure I do," he said. "That was a pretty good-sized gator, probably ten feet long. Not a really big one, mind you. But pretty good-sized."

I shook my head. If anyone had asked me, I would have bet that alligator was a world's record. Twenty feet at least.

"He didn't seem much bothered by us as I recall."

"No wonder. Those big ones, they don't have any natural enemies. Except for man. Once one of 'em gets to be that size, well, he's whipped and eaten ever'thing he's ever seen. Not afraid of the devil himself by then. I've heard of 'em chargin' cars, but I don't know if there's any truth to stories like that. People like to make things up."

I didn't have any trouble believing him. I'd dealt with a lot of lies in my time, one way or another.

"Do they ever bother people?" I said.

"Not much. Like I say, folks like to make things up, so there's stories. But as far's I know there's never been anybody in this part of the country that's got hurt. There's old Harley Tabor, but you got to disregard about half what he says and forget the other half."

"What's his story?"

"Well, Harley went bank fishin' one time in some of those lakes back in here. Had his favorite dog with him, a little border collie named Joe. He says he was fishin' along, catchin' a few bass here and there, mostly little ones, and then he got ahold of a really good one, six or seven pounds. Put up quite a fight on his little old spin cast reel, a dollar-ninety-eight Johnson, I think he said. Anyhow, he had it about whipped and was gettin' it to shore when this bull gator came up out of nowhere, like a German submarine. That's the way Harley put it—like a German submarine. I think Harley was in Europe durin' World War Two and crossed the Atlantic on troop ships a couple of times. Anyhow, the gator clamped down on that fish and wouldn't let go. Harley, bein' a stubborn type of a guy himself, wouldn't let go either."

He stopped talking and mashed out his Camel in the bottom of the boat, dug out another one, lit it.

"Made the gator mad, I guess, and it decided to go after Harley. That's the way he tells it. Says the gator came chargin' up on the bank, showin' all its teeth, makin' a funny noise like a hiss."

"Like a snake?" I said.

"Louder'n that," he said, taking a drag on his cigarette. "I've heard 'em."

"So what happened? The gator eat him?"

Fred laughed. "Not quite. But almost. Those gators can move fast when they get on the ground, faster'n a horse, a lot faster'n a man. But just for a short distance. Then it's all over. Harley said he was so scared, he broke the world's record for the hundred-yard dash. But the gator would've got him anyway if it hadn't been for the dog."

"The dog fought the gator off?" I said. It made a nice picture, like a story you might see in *Reader's Digest*, a heart-warming bit of Americana.

"Naw," Fred said. "Nothin' like that. The dog was too scared to move, so the gator stopped to eat him. Gave old Harley the lead time he needed. He said that gator didn't hardly slow down, though, just scooped up the dog in one big mouthful and kept on comin'. Harley says he's lucky to be alive today, and that he owes it all to that dog."

"You believe that?" I said.

"Ain't nobody seen that dog from that day till this."

There wasn't anything I could say to that. Fred mashed out his second Camel and stood up, the pole in his hands. He started poling the boat again, and soon we were back to where we'd started. He managed to pole us up onto the bank so that I didn't have to get wet when I stepped out.

After we'd pulled the boat completely out of the water, he said, "Well, what do you think?"

"About what?" I said, though I knew perfectly well what he meant.

"About the case. You gonna take it, or not?"

"I don't know, Fred."

In spite of what I'd seen, and in spite of Fred's obvious affection for his scaly pals, it was hard for me to take him seriously.

No one had ever hired me to find the murderer of an alligator before.

"Let's walk on over to the Jeep," he said, and we started walking, with me making a few futile swings at the mosquitoes that still buzzed around me.

"Until I read about you in the papers," he said, "I didn't even know you'd moved back to Galveston, much less what you did for a livin'."

"The papers got it a little bit mixed up," I told him. "Mostly I'm just a house painter these days. Even when I was an investigator I didn't get involved in things like what happened in Galveston."

"If you were an investigator once, you could be one again," he said. He was just as stubborn as Harley Tabor.

"Why not let the game warden do something?" I said.

"Bullshit. That Jack Burlingame ain't worth two cents. He hates gators, wouldn't care if they was all killed off."

"Aren't alligators in season anyway?"

"Sure, for the next two weeks. But you got to take 'em legally, and that means you don't leave the carcass on my land. And it means you got to have my permission to hunt on my land, and a lot of other things. Which whoever did this didn't have."

What really galled Fred was that someone had killed a gator, skinned it, and left the meat to rot right there on his property. Also, there were no signs of legal activity, which would probably have included a stake in the ground, so Fred believed that someone had shot the gator while it was swimming—and that was an illegal act.

"When I was an investigator, I usually just looked for missing people," I said. "I didn't go around looking for people who murdered alligators."

"What's the difference? If you're lookin' for somebody, you're lookin' for somebody."

"There is a difference," I said. "There are ways to trace a missing person. Somebody like you want me to find, well, it's not the same."

"Clues, huh?"

"Not exactly, but that's close enough."

The trail we were on wound through some trees and then opened out on a field. The Jeep was parked there. It was an old Willys, old enough to have been driven in Europe by Harley Tabor during the Second World War according to Fred, though I doubted it. It looked more like one of the models from the late fifties to me. Whenever it had been built, it was still reliable.

"Made in America by Americans," Fred said. "And you don't need to plug it into some damn computer to find out what's wrong with it."

We climbed in and Fred cranked it up. Then we were bouncing across the field on the way to the road.

"Well?" Fred said.

"All right," I said. "I'll give it a try. But no guarantees."

"That's good enough for me," he said between bounces.

I don't know why I accepted, really. Maybe because I didn't have any houses to paint at the moment. Maybe because I finally realized it was time to try to work my way back into the world a little bit.

"I hear they found your sister," Fred said.

"Yeah," I said. "They found her."

That, too.

▽

2

MY SISTER'S NAME was Jan. She disappeared.

That's why I went back to Galveston, trying to find her. That was what I was supposed to be good at—finding people—but I didn't find Jan. Long after giving up hope of seeing her again, I'd continued staying on the Island, hoping I'd get word of her, thinking I'd find a clue to lead me to her.

I never did.

It shook me, and I blamed myself. So I stayed on, doing odd jobs, painting houses mainly, making enough to get by, and then I got involved with a couple of childhood buddies. Dino and Ray. Dino's daughter had disappeared, and he wanted me to find her.

I did, but things didn't work out as well as they might have. Like me, Dino had been Born on the Island. BOI, most people said. And now we found ourselves locked into strange patterns that saw me give up my profession and Dino become almost a recluse.

To tell the truth, he was doing better than I was and was actually getting out of his house a bit these days. He'd stopped spending all his time watching soap operas on TV.

I'd long since given up any hope of locating Jan, or at least of finding her alive. In the Houston area, it's not so unusual for people to disappear, but sometimes they turn up later, usually not in very good condition.

That's the way it was with Jan. A couple of kids found her. Or what was left of her.

Bones, mostly. A few rags of clothing. That was all.

The kids had been out rabbit hunting in an overgrown field not too far off Interstate 45, the main highway that connects Houston and Galveston. They found the remains—that's what they called it on the TV news, "the remains"—in the middle of the field. The kids ran all the way home to tell their parents.

I heard the report that night. I always listened for things like that, and I made a note to myself to send Jan's dental records to the medical examiner's office, just in case. I did that whenever I caught a story about bodies being discovered, but so far there had been no response.

This time, there was. Not all the bones were there. They'd been disturbed by small animals, probably. But the skull was there, and the ID was positive.

They couldn't tell me how she'd died. There wasn't enough left for that. Naturally, given the location of "the remains," foul play was assumed. But it couldn't be proven.

I'd always told myself that when Jan's body was found that I'd find her killer. Some way, I would find him.

But there just wasn't any way I could do that. It could be that I already had, though I could never be sure. Last words of dying men are notoriously unreliable. At the time, I'd been sure; now, I had my doubts.

It didn't really matter. It was all in the past now, and while I was certain I'd still feel the guilt that I'd felt earlier—what if I'd kept in touch with Jan better? What if I'd tried to find her sooner?—at least it was all over.

And because it was over, it was time for me to get back out into the world, to try getting out of the self-pitying rut I was in and do something again, something besides painting houses.

It wasn't that there was anything wrong with painting. In

fact, I enjoyed it in a way. It was the kind of work that gave you quick results. You could see what you were doing, and you could tell that you were making an improvement. From day to day you could see your progress. It was even challeng-ing, in a way. You couldn't let your mind wander, and you couldn't get sloppy. And while a steady hand wasn't abso-lutely required, it helped.

In other words, it was all right, but it wasn't really what I wanted to do. It was something to pass the time, to get me through the day and pay me a little money for the time I spent. But that's all it was.

So when Fred Benton called, I was interested in spite of myself.

The business with Dino and Ray had made the Houston papers, or at least part of it had, and when Fred saw my name he remembered the little kid whose father had brought him to see the alligators. And when he saw that I was a private investigator, or at least had been one in the recent past, and that I had been involved in a case that included a murder or two, he decided to give me a call.

After all, to Fred, killing an alligator was murder, and he was willing to pay me to find the killer. It wasn't exactly the kind of job I was used to, and it certainly wasn't glamorous, but it would get me off the Island and out of the house. Maybe it would even get me interested in something besides my own problems, the way Dino's kidnapped daughter had.

Hell, it was worth a try.

I got out of the Jeep at Fred's house, a long, low, ranch-style building with a carport that had room for a Lincoln Town Car, the Jeep, a tractor, and a Ford pickup. There was a light on in the kitchen.

"Want to come in for a little nip?" Fred said.

"I think I better get back to Galveston," I said. "I have to feed my cat. He gets upset if I don't feed him."

"You're kidding me, right?" Fred was standing by the Jeep, one foot up on the little step attached to the side.

"I'm not kidding," I said.

It wasn't that Nameless got upset, really. It was more that I felt an obligation to him. There were times when I thought he was only letting me feed him to make me feel good, and I appreciated that.

"You gonna come back tomorrow?"

"I'll be here. How early should I start?"

"People around here get up early. Prob'ly a lot earlier than you do."

"I can get up early if I have to," I said.

"You don't have to. Just get here in the middle of the mornin'. I've got a lot more stuff to tell you."

"Such as?"

"Such as who might kill a gator like that. How much do you charge, anyway?"

I hadn't thought about it. Dino paid me two hundred dollars a day, plus expenses, so that's what I said. Fred was an old friend in a way, but then he had a Lincoln Town Car. I couldn't let sentiment get in the way of making money.

"Sounds about right," he said. "I'll see you in the mornin', then. You plannin' to stay here, or you gonna have to go home ever' night to feed your kitty cat?"

"It might be a good idea for me to stay here," I said. "I can get someone to feed the cat."

"You sure? I'd hate to see a kitty cat go hungry."

I was beginning to regret having said anything about the cat. It looked like Fred didn't have the same feelings for cats that he did for alligators.

"The cat'll be fine," I said.

"All right, then. If you're sure. You can stay here at the house. Mary won't mind."

Mary was his wife, a short, round woman with red hair that should've by rights had a lot of gray in it, considering her age. I guess she knew a good beautician.

"You can stay in the guest bedroom," Fred went on. "I'll have her make it up for you."

"I wouldn't want you to go to any trouble."

"You said you were gonna charge me for expenses, didn't you?"

"Yeah," I said.

"Well, I can't afford to put you up at some fancy motel, and besides, there's not one anywhere close. So you can stay here."

"That should be fine, then."

"Good. I'll see you in the mornin'." He took his foot off the step, shook hands with me to seal the deal, and started inside.

"You sure you don't want to tell me anything else tonight?" I said. "Give me something to think about?"

"You go feed your kitty cat. Get your beauty sleep. We can talk tomorrow."

"All right," I said. I walked over to where my car was parked and got in. By the time I got it started, he was in the house.

The air-conditioning in the '79 Subaru wasn't as efficient as it might have been, but after ten or twelve miles it was at least relatively cool inside when you considered the heat and humidity outside. My shirt, a short-sleeved gray sweatshirt, was beginning to feel clammy on my chest, and most of the sweat on my face had dried.

I managed to pick up a Houston oldies station on the radio and was treated to Jackie Wilson singing "Higher and Higher," probably the best song he ever did, which is saying a lot. It made me feel better just to listen to it. After his incredible falsetto faded out, I heard a flurry of cajun fiddles, and there were Rusty and Doug singing "Alligator Man," a song I hadn't heard or thought of in well over twenty years.

I wondered if it meant anything.

I took my time on the way home, and Nameless was waiting for me outside the house when I got there. He liked to prowl the neighborhood most of the night, but he always wanted in for a snack about ten o'clock. It was a lot later than that, and I wondered how long he'd been waiting.

I had hardly stopped the car before he jumped up on the hood and stalked around with his tail in the air, looking at me through the windshield.

I got out of the car. "All right. All right," I said. "Tender Vittles, coming right up."

I started for the house, and he leaped down from the hood and flashed by me to wait at the door. I had moved to a house on the western part of the Island, the very house, as a matter of fact, where we'd finally found Dino's daughter. Dino owned the house, and he had decided he'd never live there, it being too close to the actual beach and sand that some of the Island's natives liked to avoid as much as possible in a kind of reverse snobbery.

It was a very private house, surrounded by bushes and shrubs so that you could hardly see it from the road, and there were no other houses nearby. If the Island ever flooded, I'd have to get out, assuming that I got enough advance warning, but otherwise it was ideal.

It was a place where I could lose myself again, if I wanted to.

Nameless liked it, too. He liked all the trees and shrubs and the various birds and lizards he could hunt in them. He liked scouting around the mostly barren neighborhood for whatever it was that lived in places like that and that was slower than a cat. He had taken the move very well, considering that he had never really lived with me in the first place, and it had allowed him to get back to his ancient hunting heritage.

Still, he liked his packaged food. It was regular, more or less, and it didn't try to run when he bit it. I didn't think he got very much nourishment out of the birds and mice he caught, anyway. Mostly he just liked to play with them until they no longer amused him and then kill them with the casual cruelty that all cats are capable of. Then he'd bring them to the front door and lay them out for my approval.

When I thought about it, casual cruelty like that was what Fred Benton was asking me to look into. The kind of cruelty that would lead someone to kill an alligator, skin it, and leave the carcass for Fred to find, almost as if to say, Look what I did. Aren't you proud of me?

Or maybe it was a warning of some kind. It was impossible to say now, of course, but maybe it was a good sign that my mind was getting on the right wave lengths, trying to think like a hunter again.

I hoped I would be able to adjust as well as Nameless had.

I opened the door and we went in. He scooted through the living room for the kitchen, which is where his bowls were, one for food and one for water. I fed him a package of Tender Vittles Lite—Ocean Whitefish flavor— and then stood there while he ate it. If I left, he'd just come looking for me and howl until I came and stood beside him. I knew he would eventually go ahead and eat if I ignored him, but I was never quite stubborn enough to wait him out.

After he'd eaten most of the food, he got a drink. Or several drinks. He stood and lapped water until I thought he might pop, though he never had yet. I think there's something in that packaged food that makes cats thirsty, or else Nameless had a great craving for water.

When he finished drinking, he wanted back out. I went out with him and looked across the scrub to the bay. I thought about Jan, but not for long. It was time to put all that out of my mind and get on with it.

Whatever "it" was.

I looked around for Nameless, but he was long gone. I went back inside to read a little about alligators so I wouldn't look like a complete fool the next day. I thought that I surely had a book about them somewhere. I had books about nearly everything else.

That's all I'd brought with me from the last place I'd lived—books. Dino's house was furnished, mostly with garage sale items, true, but comfortable enough for me. There was a worn old couch with a brown cover, a color TV set that no longer had very true colors, a radio, a bed, a stove, a refrigerator, and even a washer and dryer. All the comforts.

There weren't any bookshelves, though, and I'd been planning to build some. I just hadn't gotten around to it yet. That meant there were books stacked everywhere. On the floor, on the couch, on the TV set, and even on the dryer. Not on the washer, though. It loaded from the top.

I'd been reading Faulkner, and I was up to *The Hamlet*. I was determined to read straight through his works, but it was going to take me a while. I was pretty sure he wouldn't mind if I interrupted my schedule to read up on alligators.

As it turned out, I didn't have much to read on the subject. All I could find was an article in an old encyclopedia set that I'd probably picked up at a library sale. There were a couple of volumes missing from the set, and I was glad the *A* volume wasn't one of them.

About all I learned was how to tell a crocodile from an alligator, which didn't matter much to me, since there weren't any crocodiles in Texas except in zoos. But in case I ever needed to know, a crocodile had a longer and more tapered snout than an alligator.

And a crocodile is mostly gray, while an alligator is mostly black. That was an interesting point, one that I already knew. It even bothered me occasionally. Who was it that came up with the idea that alligators were green? Walt Kelly?

And here was the real clincher. Crocodiles have about fifty-eight teeth. Alligators have eighty and up. Believe me, if it ever got to the tooth-counting stage, it would be too late for me to care.

There was more in the article, of course, things about where alligators lived, and about their eyes, and about what they liked to eat, which is apparently anything that comes near their mouths, including rocks, bones, dogs, cats, fish, birds, you name it. None of the information, as interesting as it was, looked to be of any use to me.

In fact, I suspected that a few hours with Fred Benton would teach me much more about gators than I would ever learn from a book, so I put the encyclopedia aside and tried to think about what to take with me and how long I might be away.

I shoved some sweatshirts into a cheap canvas bag and put in a couple of pairs of jeans with them. Underwear. Socks. A spare pair of running shoes in case I had time to go for a run while I was at Fred's place. I didn't know if the running did my trick knee any good, but I liked to think it did. As long as I didn't try to run too fast.

That was all I needed. I could throw in the shaving kit in the morning. I liked to travel light.

Then I thought about taking a pistol.

What the hell, I thought. *I won't need a pistol. What could happen that would involve shooting?*

I put the bag on the couch and went to bed.

$\triangledown$

3

I CALLED DINO the next morning at seven.

"What the hell?" he said when he finally answered the phone after the twelfth ring. He wasn't used to getting up quite so early.

"I need a little help with my cat," I said.

"Tru? Is that you, Tru?"

"Right the first time. And people say you're stupid."

"They better not say it where I can hear them, god-dammit." Dino's uncles had controlled most of the gambling and prostitution in the old days when Galveston Island was about as wide open as anything ever got in Texas. He was used to getting respect, though not from me. "You say something about a cat?"

"I thought you might want to come by here once a day and feed him," I said.

"Why the hell would I want to do that?"

"I'm going out of town. I've got a sort of a job."

"You're gonna start painting houses out of town?"

"This is a different kind of job," I told him. "More along the lines of what I used to do."

"You going looking for somebody?" I could hear the interest in his voice. Also the doubt.

19

"Not exactly," I said. "It's a murder investigation."

"Murder?" He was hooked for sure now, but I spoiled it by telling him the whole story. "Sounds crazy to me," he said. "But at least it'll get you out of town. I worry about you."

I worried about Dino, too, but he was keeping company with the mother of his daughter again, and I thought he was doing a lot better than he had been just a few months before.

"Don't worry about me," I said. "Worry about what'll happen to my cat if he doesn't get fed. You and Evelyn could drive out here and give him a bowl of Tender Vittles. It'd be a nice outing for you."

He thought about it. "What about that girl you were going around with? What was her name?"

He knew good and well what her name was, but I told him anyway. "Vicky," I said.

"Yeah. Her. What's wrong with having her do it?"

"She doesn't like cats."

"It's like that, huh?"

"Yeah, it's like that."

Dino and I have known each other a long time, since high school and before. Both of us knew I was lying about Vicky, and both of us knew that there would be no more said about it. The truth was that Vicky had decided I was too much of a brooder, that I was never going to do anything but paint houses, and that there wasn't a thing she could do to change me. She was also sure she didn't want to have any more to do with me unless I *did* change. So we weren't seeing much of each other lately.

"I guess I could do it," Dino said. He didn't sound too happy about the idea, though.

"Nameless would appreciate it," I said. "And so would I."

"Great," he said. "Just what I need. The appreciation of a cat and a crazy man."

"I'll leave the food packets in a coffee can on the porch," I said. "Right by the bowl."

"Fantastic. Nursemaid to a pussycat. What next?"

"Don't let Nameless hear you call him that."

"Call him what?"

"A pussycat."

"Just 'cause a guy's got balls on him don't mean he ain't a pussy."

"Never mind," I said. "I won't be gone long, so it won't be too tough on you."

"Wonderful. Give me a call if you need any help catching the killer."

"I'll be sure to do that," I said.

I got back to Fred Benton's place about nine o'clock the next morning. It was off the main highway, down a graveled road where the trees grew close enough to touch from the car window and the Spanish moss hung down from them in large clumps. The day was already hot and humid.

Fred was in the carport, tinkering with the engine in the Jeep. "Just checking the oil," he said when I walked over. "You had breakfast yet?"

"No," I said. "I don't usually eat it."

"What I figured. Come on in."

I followed him inside, where the air-conditioning was a welcome relief. Mary, whom I'd met the day before, was standing by an electric range, cracking eggs into a skillet.

"How many do you eat?" she said.

"Two, I guess." I didn't want to overdo it.

There was bacon on a white plate by the stove, and in a few minutes she was scraping the scrambled eggs out of the skillet onto the plate as well. Fred and I sat at a big oval table made out of some dark wood, and Mary put the plate in front of me.

"You want some toast?" she said.

"No, thanks," I said. "This is fine."

"How about a little picante sauce for those eggs?"

"That sounds great," I said, and it did. I was beginning to think I might like this job after all.

I spooned some picante onto the eggs and started eating.

Mary brought me a glass of milk. I needed it. The picante was a little hotter than I was used to.

Fred sat and watched me eat. When I finished, he said, "Now we need to talk about alligators."

Mary took my plate and rinsed it under the faucet, leaving it to sit in the sink. She wasn't going to stay around for the talk, obviously.

I pushed my chair back from the table. "OK," I said.

"I like gators," he said. "Told you that yesterday. I don't hold much with killin' 'em even if it's legal, but I can understand why the state's opened up the season on 'em again. That's all right with me. I don't—"

"Wait a minute," I said, interrupting. "*I* don't understand why the season's been opened again. I'm not even sure why it closed."

"Well, it did. Back in '69. Reopened in '84. People were about to kill all the gators off at one time, and by outlawin' all killin' the state gave 'em a chance to come back. It didn't take long. Now there's too many of 'em for some folks. They say they kill dogs and goats and no tellin' what else. Still, you got to have a license to take one, and you got to skin 'em a certain way with a certain kind of a cut, or the hides can't be sold. Legally, anyway. And they just allow a certain number to be killed ever' year. It's all controlled pretty well."

"So whoever killed that gator of yours probably didn't have a license?"

"Hell, son, I wouldn't let 'em on my land even if they did have a license."

"What about the skin?"

"It won't be sold legally. This is a case of poachin', and murder."

"And the game warden doesn't see it that way?"

"Jack Burlingame. It's not that he don't see it that way. It's just that he's lazy. Sorry as owl shit. And prob'ly scared of whoever did it."

"You think he knows?"

"I bet he has an idea or two. I know I do."

That was what I'd been waiting to hear. I had known last night that Fred had some ideas on the subject, and he'd just wanted to wait till morning to let me hear them.

"Well, give me the names, then."

"Zach Holt, for one," he said.

"Who's he?"

"He's an outlaw, that's who he is. He lives down in the river bottoms in an old run-down shack with that wife of his, and Lord knows what it is that he does to get by. Nobody can prove anything on him, but we're nearly all sure he poaches—gators, mostly."

"So if he makes his living that way, why would he insult you by leaving a carcass on your land?"

"We've had a run-in or two," Fred said.

"What does that mean?"

"Means I've seen him in town and given him a piece of my mind, that's what it means. Means I've told him I think he's a low-down skunk that lives off other people's property."

"If you don't like him, you can come right out and tell me," I said. "No need to mince your words."

"What're you talkin' about? I—oh. I get it. You're kiddin' me, right?"

"Maybe a little bit," I said.

"Well, I got to say that when I don't like a fella, especially if I think he's been doing something wrong to me or my friends, I don't mind lettin' him know about it."

"But all you've ever done is tell him. You haven't gotten into any fights or anything?"

" 'Course not. I'm too old for gettin' into fights. Now if I was a few years younger. . . ."

"It's just as well that you aren't," I said.

"Prob'ly is. That Zach is big as a bear. He'd prob'ly pull my head right off."

"Who else do you suspect?"

"I don't exactly *suspect* anybody. I'm just sayin' that these are ideas about who might've done it."

"All right. I understand. What about another idea?"

"Hurley Eckles," he said.

"Is he another poacher?"

"I didn't say Holt was a poacher. I didn't say that."

"You said—"

"I said ever'body was sure he poaches. But we can't prove it."

"OK. I see the difference. What about this Hurley Eckles?"

"He runs a little fillin' station and grocery store down at the crossroads." Fred made a gesture in the general direction with his right hand. I didn't have any idea where he was pointing, but I could find that out later. "He runs with a bunch of fellas that get into all kinds of meanness. I don't guess they're bad, exactly, but they do things."

"What kinds of things?"

"Things like killin' gators. Not that they've been caught at it, but you know what I mean. Maybe a little rustlin', too."

"Rustling? I thought that went out with Roy Rogers and Gene Autry."

"Well, you were wrong if you thought that. It still goes on all the time. It's just that nobody gets up on a horse and runs the cattle from one range to the next these days. They load 'em in trailers."

"In the movies they always ran them over the rocky ground so no one could follow them," I said. It was a trick that had impressed me when I was a kid, and it must have impressed the writers, too. They all used it.

Fred laughed. "There's not a lot of rocky ground around here to run 'em on, in the first place. But anyway, Hurley and the boys are into stuff like that."

"But nobody's caught them in the act?"

"That's about the size of it."

I didn't like it. Here were Fred's two main suspects, and neither one of them, as far as he knew, had ever really been caught at anything illegal. They were both suspected of doing things, or if suspected was the wrong word, they were rumored to have done things. But exactly *what* things no one could say for sure.

It sounded as if Hurley Eckles was guilty of running with a bad crowd—if anybody had any evidence against the crowd, which I doubted—and Zach Holt was guilty of living in a run-down shack. As far as I could see, especially considering my own residence, that wasn't a crime, and it didn't lead naturally to killing alligators.

"You got any more ideas?"

"That's about it," Fred said. "It's one of them two, you can bet on it."

It wasn't anything I'd want to lay my life's savings on, but it was a place to start. That's about all it was.

"Is that carcass still there?" I said. "Where you found it?"

"Yeah. I left it. Just as a reminder."

"Let's go look at it," I said.

The Jeep carried us down into the bottom land again, but to a different area from the one we'd visited last night. I didn't know how much land Fred owned, so I asked him.

"Little over three thousand acres," he said. "Ever' bit of it just as wild as this."

We were passing through a thick stand of trees with just about room for the Jeep to get through them. It was a trail that Fred had obviously used before. Suddenly he braked the Jeep to a halt.

"Look over there," he said.

I looked in the direction he indicated, but I didn't know what to look for and therefore didn't see anything except more trees and deeper shadows.

"Deer," he said.

I saw them then, two does standing absolutely still and watching us from the cool shade of the farther trees.

"I got a lot of deer in here," Fred said. "I don't allow any huntin' of *them*, either."

"I thought you had to keep them thinned out, keep the herd from getting too big and starving."

He shifted the Jeep into gear and we trundled off. "That might be true in most cases," he said. "But not here. I plant feed for 'em in the winter, and they got plenty. I don't notice any of 'em dyin' off."

We came out of the trees and into the bright sun, and before us was a marshy lake like the one we'd put the boat into last night. The water was choked with cattails and rushes, and hundreds of birds flew up out of them with a loud beating of wings when we drove up. The Jeep's engine must have scared them. It looked like something from an old Tarzan movie, or maybe something from a Louisiana swamp epic.

Fred drove down a very slight incline and then turned right onto the heavy earthen dam that held the water in check. "It's down on the end of the dam," he said.

A few days in the sun and heat hadn't made the carcass very pleasant. I could smell the unforgettable sweetish stink of rot as soon as Fred stopped the Jeep.

Not only was the carcass beginning to rot, it looked as if hunks of it had been torn away by other gators or by something that I didn't even want to know about.

"Back in the old days, over in East Texas, there used to be old boys'd go out into the marshes for months at a time," Fred said. "They'd kill gators and skin 'em and leave the carcasses right there in their camp. I've heard about how the buffalo hunters used to smell, but I bet they didn't have a thing on the gator skinners."

I wouldn't have bet with him. My nose told me that there wasn't much doubt that he was right.

"I don't suppose there were any tracks around here?" I said.

"Not a one. Hadn't rained in about a week, and this old ground gets hard as a rock in that length of time, at least where it drains. Otherwise, it stays sticky as gumbo."

We got out of the Jeep and walked over to the decaying gator. I tried to breathe through my mouth.

"How do you think whoever did this got in here?" I said.

"Just like we did. Drove in. Or, hell, they could've walked."

"Wouldn't they have to pass by your house?"

"Nope. There's plenty of ways in and out of here if you know your way around. I didn't find any cut fences, if that's on your mind, but I don't think that matters, either. They could get keys to the gate locks if they really tried."

I looked out over the marshy water. I didn't see any alligators. "So it could've been anyone at all."

"Sure it could. But I'd lay my money on Zach Holt or Hurley Eckles."

"I guess I'd better talk to them, then," I said, just as the first rifle bullets smacked into the darkening body of the dead gator.

4

A DARK CLOUD of flies spewed up from the rotting body, humming like an amplified dial tone. Fetid meat splattered away from the bones as the bullet smacked into the carcass. The sharp crack of the rifle followed the splatting noise almost immediately, and more birds flew up out of the cattails, cawing and squawking.

I didn't blame them. I felt a little like squawking and cawing myself. A piece of the stinking body meat had struck my shirt, and it clung there as I batted at it with my hand, trying to brush the smell of death off me while at the same time running in a low crouch back toward the Jeep.

Fred was a little bit ahead of me, having been standing behind me when the shot was fired. He stopped suddenly when a bullet plowed the dirt in front of him, but for an old man he was pretty shifty. Almost without hesitation, he turned to his right and plunged down the low-lying dam and into the water below.

I was right behind him all the way. I wasn't thinking of alligators or snakes or anything else that might be in there. I just wanted away from those bullets.

We splashed into the water, our feet releasing bubbles of gas that had been trapped on the bottom by decaying vegetation. The bubbles rose and popped, releasing their chemical-plant odor into the air. I hardly noticed. I was busy falling down and getting my head below the level of the dam, which seemed even lower when you were trying to use it as a barricade against rifle shots.

A couple more bullets whistled by over our heads. I don't suppose that I actually heard them whistling, but it seemed that way. I know for sure that I heard them ripping through the cattails behind me.

The water was unpleasantly warm and slimy with algae, and a swarm of gnats hummed in front of my eyes and flew in my face. Rifle bullets didn't bother them.

My clothes were soaked and clinging to my body. I found myself wishing illogically that I had brought my pistol, though I knew that it would be no good at all against a rifle. At least I would be able to shoot back and make noise with it. As it was, all I could do was lie there hoping an alligator didn't bite my ass off.

I turned my head to look at Fred, who was no more comfortable than I was. "I've got a nasty little feeling there's something going on here that you didn't tell me about, Fred," I said.

He opened his mouth to answer, but the rifle cracked twice more. The birds were flying in circles now, making a raucous noise that reminded me of a certain Hitchcock movie. Occasionally something would plop into the water nearby. That was all I needed—for a bird to shit on me. Thinking that, I began to laugh at myself. Bird shit was a whole hell of a lot better than getting shot or eaten by a gator.

But not by much.

We lay there for what seemed like a long time, not saying anything more. I looked at my black plastic runner's watch, determined that I wasn't going to move for thirty minutes after the last shot. The time passed very slowly, but at least I wasn't shit on. It was close a time or two, but that was all.

The birds were more impatient than I was. After about fifteen minutes, they began to settle back down into the reeds and the rushes, and after twenty or so minutes they were quiet again.

After twenty-five minutes, Fred poked me in the arm with his finger. I looked at him and he pointed beyond and behind me to a group of large green lily pads that lay smoothly on the water. In front of them were the eyes and the snout of a gator.

I decided that thirty minutes being an arbitrary and artificial limit, the twenty-five or -six that had already passed were certainly enough. I got rapidly out of the water and sprinted for the Jeep, sliding to a stop behind it, but there were no more shots.

Fred followed more slowly, and I realized that he wasn't afraid of the gator and had been pointing it out only as a form of silent conversation. That was all right with me, but all the same I felt better out of the water, though I still wasn't especially eager to stick my head up over the top of the Jeep.

So I sat with my back braced against the front wheel and let some of the water from my clothes drip off onto the ground. Sitting out of the water in soaking jeans and a sweatshirt is even more uncomfortable than sitting *in* the water, but at least there weren't any alligators up there.

Not yet, anyway. I looked over to the lily pads, but the snout was gone.

Fred crawled around me and leaned against the back wheel. "That's more excitement than an old man needs," he said.

"It's more than any man needs," I said. "So let's get back to what I started to say earlier."

"What's that?" Fred said.

"Come on, Fred. Don't give me that senile bit. You know damn well what I mean."

He pulled a hangdog look. "I guess I do," he said.

"Well, what about it?"

"You may be right."

"*May* be? Some guy starts shooting real bullets at us, I get rotten alligator meat on my shirt, I spend a half hour in stinking, slimy water waiting for a live gator to eat me, birds shit on me—"

"Didn't no birds shit on you. I was watchin', and didn't no birds shit on you."

"You're right," I said. "I'm sorry. I was getting a little bit carried away, which I sometimes tend to do when people start shooting at me for no reason at all that I know about but which I suspect someone else knows about and should've told me about."

I had to stop to catch my breath. Obviously I was still a little bit carried away. I leaned back against the tire and tried to breathe normally and calmly.

"I don't blame you for bein' upset," Fred said. "It's more to the story than meanness and poachin'. I hoped that's all there was to it, and so that's why I told you that."

It was about as close to an apology as I was likely to get from Fred Benton. He was an independent old cuss, and he wasn't used to saying that he was sorry to anyone. Maybe he really had hoped to avoid telling me all that was involved. That was true in a lot of cases. People never want to tell the whole truth until it's absolutely forced on them. Sometimes not even then. Ask Richard Nixon. Ask Ronald Reagan.

"OK," I said. "I understand. But now there's a brand-new ball game going on, and somebody's not playing by the rules. At least not by the polite rules. So maybe you better tell me the whole thing."

"I will," he said. "You don't reckon that whoever took those shots is sneakin' around tryin' to get closer to us, do you?"

I took a quick look to my right and my left and didn't see anything suspicious. Of course I hadn't seen anything before the first shots, either.

"You wouldn't be trying to stall me, would you, Fred?"

"I guess I would. Not on purpose, though."

That was a new one on me, and I said so.

"I mean that I want to tell you, but I don't know how. I don't even know *what*," he said.

I took a deep breath. "Just try starting at the beginning and working through it to the end."

"I don't know if I can do that," he said. Then he saw the look on my face. "I'm not tryin' to be dumb about it, and that's the truth. Let's put it this way. The dead gator's not the first thing that's happened."

"Not the first," I said. "Well, that's a start. Now tell me what you mean."

"I don't know. I told you that."

The conversation was going nowhere, so I tried to take control of it. "Other things have happened, like the alligator thing, but you don't know why, and you don't know who's doing them. Is that it?"

He shook his head. "That's it. That's it exactly."

I thought things over for a minute. Whoever had been doing that shooting could probably have killed us as easily as not. Thinking back on it, it seemed that maybe someone was shooting more to scare us than to kill us.

If that was the case, it had worked very well, at least as far as I was concerned.

And the dead alligator? Some sort of warning, like the shots? Or a threat?

"Tell me about the other things," I said.

"They weren't as bad as this, not near as bad as this. In fact, I didn't really think that much about 'em, not till I found that dead gator."

"Name one thing," I said, trying to keep the frustration I was feeling out of my voice. The air was so thick that my clothes weren't drying, and they hung on me like damp wash. There had to be something I could do to get a straight answer, but sounding upset wasn't it.

"My dog died," Fred said after a second or two.

I just waited. What could I say to that?

"He was old. Hell, he must've been eighteen years old. He'd been lookin' poorly for the last year or two, and so I didn't really think anything was funny when he died. Now I wonder if he might've been poisoned, though."

"But you didn't at first?"

"Naw. He just died. I didn't see it or anything like that. I just came out one mornin', and there he was in the yard. Not a mark on him. I figured it was just old age, and he just keeled over."

"OK," I said. "That's one thing. What came next?"

"I guess it was the phone calls."

"What phone calls?"

"That's a hard one to explain," he said. "They was just phone calls."

"What about the caller? What did he say? Who was he asking for?"

"That's hard to say. The phone would ring, and we'd answer it, but there wouldn't ever be anybody on the other end, at least not that we could hear. We'd say 'hello' over and over, but there wasn't ever any answer."

"What time of day did the calls come?"

"Most anytime. Day or night. Sometimes real late. Sometimes real early. All during the day."

"They've stopped?"

"Yeah. They stopped right before the noises started."

"The noises?" I said. There was a pattern, all right, and I'd bet that Fred had seen it from the beginning.

"At night. Late," Fred said. "Noises like animals callin' or clankin' noises like somebody was beatin' on an oil drum with a tree limb, or a chain sometimes."

"Did you ever investigate the noises, try to see who was making them?"

"Oh, sure. I'd get up, look around for my gun, get some pants on, find my flashlight. But by the time I'd ever get outside, whoever was makin' the noises would be cleared out."

I looked over at him. "And it never occurred to you that someone might be deliberately harassing you?"

His old blue eyes were a little watery, but they were guileless. "I thought it was prob'ly kids," he said. "You know how kids are."

"But you don't think kids killed the alligator."

"And skinned it like that? That's a professional job. Nope, kids didn't do that."

I wished I hadn't mentioned the alligator. Now I could smell it again, and it wasn't doing my stomach any good. In fact, along with being shot at, that smell was almost enough to cause me to lose the breakfast I'd eaten.

"Is there anything else you forgot to tell me? Any more little incidents you forgot to mention?"

"That's about it. Seems like things are gettin' worse, though."

"At least we're alive," I said.

Then I thought about that. The shots were probably just a warning, like everything else Fred had finally told me about, all of which were more threatening than actually harmful. Except to the dog and the gator.

"Fred," I said, "I took this job because of sentiment and nostalgia, more or less. I didn't need a job, and I haven't done one by my own choice for a long time now. No money's changed hands yet. So I could just get you to give me a ride back to your house where I can get my bag and drive back to Galveston. That would probably be the smart thing for me to do. But I won't."

I paused and thought about it. "*Maybe* I won't. I'm about ready for some clean, dry clothes, and I don't think our shooter's out there anymore, so I'm going to let you give me that ride. While we're on the way, you think about how bad you want me to find your gator killer, and then you think about what you still haven't told me about whatever it is that you're involved in. Then I'll let you know whether I'm still on the job."

I stood up and looked around. No one shot at me.

Fred got up then and gave me a hurt look. "I didn't know all that other stuff was tied in. I still don't know it."

"I don't know it, either," I said. "But I'd say it's pretty certain. One or two things, well, that could be explained as random happenings. But everything you've told me about? No way."

We got in the Jeep. Fred started it and backed down the
dam to the trail we'd come in on. He did a quick flip of the
wheel and got us started in the right direction, then spun
the tires and flung dirt when we took off.

Fred had me throw my wet clothes in the washer. "I'll take
care of 'em," he said. "No need to involve Mary in any of
this."

"Yes there is," I said. "You may not think so, but she's in
this thing just as much as you are. Whatever it is."

I was feeling a little better, but not good enough to let him
off the hook. I'd been to my room, a very nice one, with a
double bed and carpet on the floor, and getting into dry jeans
and a dry shirt had improved my outlook and calmed me
down. Despite my recent escapade in Galveston, I still
wasn't used to being shot at, and it took me a while to get
back to what passed for normal in my case.

"So why don't you tell me what it is," I said.

'Let's go in the living room,' Fred said.

He led me to a large room that most people would have called
a den. It had paneled walls and a hardwood floor, with throw
rugs here and there. The rugs were cowhide, some with the
hair still on them, and they added to the rustic look of the
room, the walls of which were hung with Remington prints
and two rifle racks holding two shotguns and a thirty-aught-
six. There was a small bookshelf on one wall crammed with
Louis L'Amour paperbacks and the Time-Life series of books
about the Old West. In the center of the room was a huge
leather-covered couch. Fred walked over to it and sat down.

There were three or four wooden chairs in the room, their
bottoms covered with cowhide. I pulled one of them over by
the couch so that I could look at Fred while we talked.

For a good while, he didn't say anything.

Neither did I. It was cool in there, and I could hear Mary
banging around among the pots and pans in the kitchen. It
all seemed very safe and normal, and I was willing to wait.
For a few minutes, at least.

It was a little longer than that, and I was beginning to get uncomfortable in the hard-backed chair. I was more used to slumping than sitting up straight.

"I guess it's the land," Fred finally said. "That's got to be it; I can't think of anything else."

"The land," I said, just to encourage him.

"I don't want to sell it, is the thing," he said.

"Who wants you to?"

"Hard to say."

"Now don't start up with that again," I said. "There's got to be somebody, and somebody has a gun."

"Rifle," Fred said.

"Right, rifle."

We looked at each other.

Fred looked away first, but I didn't feel particularly proud. I didn't feel like I'd won anything.

"It's mostly a rumor," he said.

"What kind of rumor?"

He sighed and leaned back on the couch, putting one leg over the other. "There's a rumor—just a rumor—that the state wants to buy up a big passel of land down here. Now you got to think about that. This land's not good for much except to grow things on, rice mostly, or just to leave in its natural state. This close to Houston, there's not just a whole lot left that *is* natural."

"And the state wants the land, right?"

"That's the rumor."

"What for? Does the rumor say?"

"A state park. Big one."

"What's wrong with that? Wouldn't it leave the land the way you like it? In its natural state?"

"Sure it would."

"So what's wrong with that?"

"Nothin's wrong with that, if it's true. But it may not be true. What if somebody wants the land for a nuclear power plant or something like that? The whole thing's just a rumor."

"I'm not sure I get the point of all this anyway," I said. "Who cares what you do with your land?"

"A lot of folks, since I've let it be known that I won't sell. See, if I don't sell mine, they don't get to sell theirs. Mine's the key to the whole thing, according to the story."

Now I could see the problem. "And I take it that Zach Holt and Hurley Eckles own land that touches yours and they're tied in to the deal that way."

"You got it."

"But they can't be all. There must be others."

"You want a list?"

I did.

5

My THEORY WAS that the state didn't operate under a cloak of secrecy. If the state wanted the land, they'd let it be known. Of course, that wasn't always the case. If the facts became known too soon, the land values would skyrocket, and the speculators would be coming out of the marshes by the boatload.

And it didn't take much to start a rumor about money in these hard economic times. That was the kind of rumor that everyone would listen to and that everyone would take seriously because everyone would want to believe it. There were people living all around Fred Benton's land, but the nearest town was fifteen miles away, and I was sure that all Fred's neighbors could visualize the potent economic effects of a state park in their backyards. They wouldn't have to strain their imaginations too hard to see the dollar signs, and there would naturally be some resentment if they thought he was holding things back.

I wasn't sure that was the reason for what was going on, but it was the best I could come up with. Fred wasn't going to help me much more. I should have stuffed my clothes in the bag and gone back to the Island, but now I'd been shot at and I was mad. It was a silly game, but I didn't want whoever had fired that rifle to think I was that easy to get rid of.

I ate lunch—tuna salad—with Fred and Mary and then drove to the crossroads store, where Fred assured me I would find Hurley Eckles. The store was a little over two miles from Fred's house, down graveled roads that wound under huge oak and pecan trees, but it was easy to find.

It was an old wooden building with a huge stack of worn-out tires beside it. On the faced white paint of the building's side, the words FLATS FIXED had been painted in black letters by some unsteady hand. I'd known a cosmetic surgeon once, a man who specialized in breast enlargements, who'd wanted to use the same slogan. I'd discouraged him.

Most of the rest of the side of the building was covered with hubcaps of all sizes and descriptions. Some were heavily dented, and some were even rusting. Most of them looked as if they had been hanging there for years, though there were a couple of fairly shiny ones.

There were two almost new gas pumps in front of the store, and beside them was another hand-painted sign that indicated the price of gas to be around twenty-five cents more per gallon than it was in town. A third sign said that there were TIRES FOR SALE, and I saw a shed built onto the side of the store where the mounting and balancing equipment was kept.

Two men sat in chairs in front of the store, with the chairs tipped back to lean against the wall. They looked vaguely familiar, and they watched me without curiosity as I pulled up and stopped.

I got out of the car and walked in the store without speaking to them. It was a little cooler inside than out, probably because it was darker. Hurley Eckles didn't go in much for lighting effects. There was nobody in the store.

I went back outside. There was a big red and white Coke machine beside the two men in the chairs, and I rummaged around in my pocket until I came up with enough change. There were no Big Reds in the machine, so I slipped in the coins and pushed the button for a caffeine-free Coke. There was a clanking noise, and the familiar red and white can of a Classic Coke fell into the trough at the bottom of the machine.

The two men laughed as I looked at the can. "Don't matter which button you push," the one nearest me said. "All we got in that machine's the old Coke. Don't nobody from around here drink any other kind."

I pulled up the tab on the can and looked the men over. The one who had spoken to me was short and squat and looked a little like a frog. He was wearing an old fedora that might have been gray when it was new but was now almost green with age, grease, and much creasing and bending. In spite of the heat and humidity, he was wearing a long-sleeved blue work shirt and overalls. The shirt was stained with sweat under the arms. The sun glinted on his wireless glasses. He spit a stream of snuff in the dirt.

The other man was taller, as far as I could tell with both of them seated, and definitely thinner. He had a foxy face and bad teeth, and his thinning hair was combed in a widow's peak. He looked like the older of the two, but not by much. They were both around fifty, at a guess.

While I was studying them, they were looking at me. I took a swallow of the Coke and waited for one of them to make the first move.

It took a while. After I'd almost finished the Coke, the squat one said, "You new to the area?"

"I'm looking for somebody," I said. There was no trash can to put the empty in, so I held it in my hand.

"Who might that be?" he asked.

"Fella named Hurley Eckles."

"Well, you found him. What might I do for you?"

The other man didn't say a word, just sat there staring at me. I was beginning to wonder if he could speak at all.

"My name's Truman Smith," I said. "I was looking at land in this neck of the woods, and I heard you might have some for sale."

Eckles leaned forward, letting the legs of the chair touch

the snuff-stained ground. "I might. I might even sell this here store to the right customer."

"I'm not looking to get into the retail business," I said. "I'm just interested in land."

He looked over at my car. The little gray Subaru sat there as if it were slightly ashamed of itself. The dent in the bumper seemed to enlarge even as we watched.

Then he looked back at me. I was in clean clothes, but the clothes consisted of a pair of faded jeans and an old orange and white UT sweatshirt. I guess I didn't look a lot like a real estate tycoon, and the Casio watch didn't help any. I should have been wearing a Rolex.

"Just what kind of land you looking to buy?" he said at last.

"Well, I've been talking to Fred Benton—"

"That horse turd." Eckles's voice came out hard and flat. He was apparently no more fond of Fred than Fred was of him.

"Uh . . . horse turd?" I said.

"I didn't stutter, did I? Horse turd. That's what he is. Always has been."

"You don't think I can put much faith in his real estate advice then?"

"Lemme tell you somethin', Mr. . . . Smith, is it?"

I nodded.

"Lemme tell you about Mr. Fred Benton. He don't give a damn 'bout anybody but hisself. If he thought he could skin you in a land deal, why he'd do it in a New York minute. He didn't try to sell you any of his own land, did he?"

I didn't know what to say, so I decided to wing it. "As a matter of fact, he did."

"Sure he did. Fella, I don't know you very well, so I can't say you're a liar, but I believe you're talkin' through your asshole."

"Uh . . . "

"First place, Fred don't own no land. Ever'body knows that. Second place, if he did own it, he wouldn't sell it. Third place, you look about as much like a real estate speculator as Temp's ass." He glanced at the man beside him who still had nothing to say but who was grinning now. Hurley sent another stream of snuff to the ground.

"To tell the truth," I said, "I—"

"To tell the truth, I don't think Temp and I want to talk to you anymore," Hurley said. "Why don't you just get in your funny-lookin' little Jap car and get outta here."

It was my fault. I'd gone into it like an amateur. It had been too long since I'd done anything like this, and I'd botched it good.

I didn't think it would help now to tell him the real reason I was there, considering his feelings about Fred, so I thought I might as well do as he suggested.

When I got over to the car, I tossed the Coke can in through the open window. Then I got in and drove away. As I looked back in the rearview mirror, I could see them sitting there, not moving. And then I realized who they had reminded me of. If Bartles and Jaymes ever came to the Texas swamplands, they'd look just like Hurley and Temp.

It was too soon to go back to Fred's, so I drove around a while, trying to get the feel of the country and see what I could see. There wasn't much, unless you were a fan of trees, which I wasn't, not especially. There were houses here and there, but nothing that looked like a settlement, just the scattered houses of people who hadn't quite given in to the urge that seemed to compel most of us to live in cities, or at least in towns.

Sometimes it was hard to remember that there were still people like that, people who actually preferred to live alone and apart, to buy their groceries at a store like Hurley's instead of at the supermarket and who probably hadn't driven on a freeway more than once or twice in their lives, if they ever had.

Of course, even here you could smell the chemical plants on certain days, days when the wind was blowing just right and passed over one of the big plants in Deer Park or Texas

City or in any number of other places on the coast. Take a deep breath and you could get a whiff. You might not think about it long, or you might wonder briefly what you'd smelled, but you'd notice it, all right. Out here, though, you could tell yourself that it didn't really matter. And maybe it didn't.

Then again, maybe it did. It wasn't any of my business, though, and I put the thought out of my mind. Or maybe it was driven out by the sight of the Oldsmobile with a flat tire.

It was off to the side of the road, half in the ditch, not a good spot to try jacking it up. Unfortunately, there wasn't any other place, and a man in a white shirt and slacks was sweating over the jack handle. He'd put his blue sport coat on the fender of the car while he worked.

I stopped behind him and got out. "Trouble?" I said.

It was a stupid remark, and the man gave me the look I deserved. "I guess you could say that," he told me.

He was a big man, looking a little like a weight lifter who'd gone to seed, or maybe just a big man who worked out just enough to keep a little tone. His neck was short and thick, giving the impression that he didn't really have one, and I wondered if he wore a tie with his jacket. If he did, it wasn't lying on the car.

"My name's Truman Smith," I said. I put out my hand. "Maybe I can give you some help."

He took my hand in his own, which was sweaty and huge. It was like shaking hands with a hot gorilla. "Gene Ransome," he said. He shook gently and let go.

I looked at his other hand. There was a Presidential Rolex on the wrist above it. He looked more like a speculator than I did, though he didn't have the face for it. His nose had been broken at least once, and his black hair grew low on his brow, giving him a thuggish look.

"Maybe you can help, all right," he said. He should have sounded like Sheldon Leonard, but he sounded more like a midwestern newscaster. "This thing's sitting in a precarious spot."

We looked the situation over and decided that he should let the jack down and drive up on the road. I'd watch for cars and flag anybody down before there was a wreck. The car needed to be level, and there was no way to get it level except right on the main road.

After we decided that and he moved the car, it didn't take long to change the tire.

"I know a place where they fix flats," I said.

"Hurley's? Yeah, I know him. I'll take it there. Thanks."

He seemed like an odd sort to be in this area and to know Hurley. "You a salesman?" I said.

He smiled, showing a set of slightly damaged choppers. One at least was missing. "That's right. I know a lot of folks in this area."

"You know Fred Benton?"

"Benton? Sure, sure. I know him. He a friend of yours?"

"Sort of," I said.

"A good guy. Well, I gotta get this flat to Hurley's and get it fixed. Thanks for the help."

"Sure," I said. I watched him get in his car. Then I got in the Subaru and followed him to a turnaround, where I passed him. He headed back in the direction of Hurley's. There was something about him that bothered me, but it was nothing definite.

I drove a little longer, and then I realized that I was doing nothing more than aimless rambling. Detection wasn't any part of it. There was no use doing any more driving, so I turned back toward Fred's.

When I got there, there was a black and white sheriff's department car parked in the yard.

I got out of the car and walked to the back door, tapping on the door frame. I didn't want to barge in on anything, but at the same time I was pretty curious about what might be going on.

Mary came to the door. "Come in, Truman. You don't have to knock."

"I didn't want to interrupt," I said.

"Oh, it wouldn't be an interruption. This is about you, too."

Fine, I thought. Just what I need. The sheriff.

It wasn't the sheriff, though. It was Deputy Jackson, or as he put it, "Deppidy Norm Jackson, Mr. Smith."

I shook his hand, which was like shaking with a tree branch. Jackson was thin and wiry. Maybe skinny was the word. He looked as if he wore a size twenty-eight belt. He had on a khaki uniform, and he wore a pistol on his belt. It looked like a .38.

He and Fred were in the room with the couch. They had both stood up when I came in, and after Jackson had introduced himself, Fred told me what was going on.

"I called Deppidy Jackson right after you left," he said. "I didn't figure there was much he could do about it, but by God a man ought not to get shot at on his own land and not tell the law about it."

Jackson had pale blue eyes, so pale they were almost white. "We drove down there to where y'all got shot at," he said. "Walked over to the woods to see if the shooter left any of his brass behind him, but we didn't get lucky enough to find anything. Didn't really expect we would. That's a lot of woods."

He looked at me as if expecting some sort of response. I didn't have one, so he went on.

"Guess you know all about the dead gator back in there."

"I saw him," I said.

"Well, it ain't a felony to kill one. I killed one myself once upon a time, or me and my brother did. We weren't no more than a couple of kids. We were gonna make us a pair of shoes. Woulda made boots, I guess, if the gator'd been big enough, which he wasn't. We didn't get to make the shoes, even, but that wasn't 'cause of the gator. It was 'cause of our daddy. He caught us with that gator and whipped our butts till they was raw as liver. You can bet that was the last time I ever thought about killin' a gator."

He looked as though he thought a good whipping was all

that a gator killer deserved, and I could see by glancing at
Fred that he didn't have a very high opinion of "Deppidy"
Jackson.

"What about shooting at two men with a high-powered
rifle?" I said.

"How do you mean?" He looked at me with those icy pale
eyes.

"I mean, you think a whipping's good enough punish-
ment for that crime?"

"I guess the law says different on that one," he said. "I'll
do what I can about it, but there's no traces that we could
find of whoever did it. They must've walked in there, 'cause
there ain't no tire marks." He paused and looked at Fred.
"Least none that we could find. We couldn't even find what
tree they was in."

I hadn't thought about that, but it was logical. Whoever
had shot at us had been shooting from a good angle; in
country that flat the person almost certainly must have been
in a tree. In fact, I hadn't been thinking at all. When the
shots were fired, I wanted to get under cover, and that was
the only thing on my mind.

"We'll be lookin' into this, but I can't make any promises,
that's all I'm sayin'. No clues. No nothin'. Unless you two want
to tell me the names of anybody that'd want to shoot you."

"I'm new here, myself," I said. "As far as I know, no one
even knows I'm around."

"I guess your list would be too long," Jackson said, looking
at Fred. "I hear a lot of folks've got it in for you lately."

"Then you prob'ly know who they are," Fred said. "I'm
not makin' any lists."

"That's all right, then," the deputy said. "Just don't expect too much." He looked at me. "And you try to keep outta
trouble here. I know Mr. Benton's hired you to find out who
killed his gator, and I guess there's nothin' wrong with you
tryin' to do that, not that I can think of right off, there's not.
But people around in here don't take too much to strangers.
I'd hate to have a murder case on my hands."

I wondered if he was referring in some oblique way to the morning's shooting or if he was just giving me some kind of standard warning.

"I won't bother anyone," I said. "Not unless somebody bothers me first."

"That'd be good. Folks'll leave you alone if you leave them alone." Jackson walked over to an end table where his gray cowboy hat was sitting. He picked it up and settled it on his head. "I'll let you know if I find out anything about that shooter, Mr. Benton," he said.

Fred walked him out of the room, and I sat on the couch. When Fred came back, I said, "You really think he's going to be any help?"

"No need for me to lie about it," Fred said, scratching his head. "I don't think he can help at all. The law in this county don't do too much that they don't have to do. And I don't want you to think I'm buttin' into your business. I know you can do what I asked you to do. It's just that I thought the law ought to know that somebody's shooting guns around here and things might get dangerous."

"Rifles," I said. "Not guns."

He grinned. "Yeah," he said. "Rifles."

▽

6

I TOLD FRED that Hurley Eckles didn't like him.

"I coulda told you that," he said.

"He also didn't think I looked much like a real estate speculator," I said. "I should have tried another approach."

Fred looked me over. "You don't look like much of anything," he said, "except maybe an out-of-work house-painter."

I didn't know how to bring up the next point, so I just said it flat out. "He said you didn't own any land. He said everybody around here knew that. *I* didn't know it."

Fred looked sheepish. "He's telling the truth, I guess. Technically, he's telling the truth."

I wasn't too sure about the difference between the technical truth and the other kind. "Maybe you'd better explain that," I said.

"Mary owns the land. It's all in her name. She inherited it not long after we got married, and, well, her daddy didn't like me very much. Thought I was just a snot-nosed kid with no sense." He paused, looking back into a past I couldn't see. "He coulda been right. Anyway, he made sure to put it in the will that if Mary died before I did, the land wouldn't go to me. It'd go to our kids. Hell, I'd've given it to the kids anyway."

"You have kids?" I said.

"Two. Boy and a girl."

"Maybe you'd better tell me about them."

"Why? They ain't in on this."

"They could be."

One thing I'd learned was that you never knew who was involved in what until the whole affair was sorted out. As someone—Yogi Bear? Yogi Berra?— is supposed to have said, it isn't over till it's over. Or something like that.

"Well, they ain't," Fred said. "You can be sure of that. Gil's in Tokyo, teachin' for the University of Maryland. Terri's in the army, stationed in Alaska. I don't think either one of 'em's interested enough in this land to do a thing about it. They got other lives."

"But you're interested enough," I said.

"What's wrong with that? What's mine is Mary's and what's hers is mine. This is a community property state, but it'd be that way with us anyway. Always has been. I got lucky enough in oil leases to buy this place twice over if I wanted to, but I've always felt like I owned it."

"I was just wondering," I said.

"Well, you don't have to wonder."

"But if Mary wanted to sell the land to the state for a park. . . ."

"She wouldn't want to. There's no need for you to talk like that. She wants what I want."

I noticed that his face was getting a little red, as if he'd shaved it too close. I decided to change the subject, but to have a private talk with his wife later.

"What about this Zach Holt?" I said. "Is there still time for me to talk to him today?"

"He's not far," Fred said.

He told me how to get there, and I went back out to the Subaru. It was still summer, so the days were fairly long. I would have time to talk to Holt and get back before dark even if we had a long conversation. I thought it might be a good idea this time to tell the simple truth, that I was looking into the illegal killing of an alligator, rather than to try some cover that I wasn't suited for.

When I thought about it, I felt a little funny. I could almost hear myself: Mr. Holt? I'm Truman Smith. I'd like to ask you a few questions about a dead alligator.

Maybe it wouldn't be as bad as I thought.

I drove some more on the back roads, looking at the trees and listening to the birds and the insects. Since the air conditioner wasn't working as well as it should have, I had the window down, and the warm late-afternoon breeze had an almost pleasant feel. Fall was a long way off, but there was something in the air, something I couldn't name or identify, that let me know the season would eventually change. You could feel things like that here, away from the noise and the smell of the cars and the factories and the refineries. As I got close to Holt's house, I could smell the river, a heavy damp smell that let me know there was water nearby. A lot of water.

The house wasn't exactly a shack, as Fred had called it, but it wasn't far off. There was a 1971 Ford up on blocks in the yard, most of its body covered with reddish rust. The wheels were there, but the tires were missing. Or maybe not. There were several tires lying in the thick grass and weeds of the yard. One of them might have fit the Ford's wheels. Not all of them, however. One of them was a tractor tire.

There was a gray tomcat asleep on top of the car, and I thought of Nameless. I hoped Dino would remember to feed him.

There was a small chicken coop a few yards from the house, but the wire was in poor repair. Two chickens, one white, one red, pecked in the yellowing grass beside the Ford, seemingly unintimidated by the presence of the cat. Before long, they would be going to roost.

The sun was a big red ball above the treetops, and the shadows fell long across the yard. I got out of the Subaru and slammed the door. The cat raised his head to look at me, then sat up and started to groom himself. The chickens pecked on, undisturbed.

Nothing else was disturbed, either, which bothered me a little. There was no sound of a TV set playing in the house, no noise of a radio. I could hear the frogs down by the river; I could hear the insects humming in the grass and the birds calling in the trees. But there was no sound from the house.

The house was old and unpainted, made of wood and set up on concrete blocks in case the river rose. The windows had all their glass, and I could see electric lines running from the house to the ones strung along the road, but there was no evidence of care about the place. No one ever cut the grass. A faint odor hung in the air, reminding me of the dead gator I had sniffed earlier. I looked over my shoulder in a nervous reaction, as if I might be expecting rifle shots.

No shots came, however, and I walked toward the house. When I passed the Ford, the cat ran down the windshield and across the hood, then jumped to the ground and disappeared around a corner of the house. The chickens clucked loudly and headed in the direction of the coop.

In front of the wooden door on the house, there was a ragged and rusty screen with cotton balls stuffed in a couple of the smaller holes. I pulled back the screen and knocked. It was an awkward angle to open the door from, since I was standing on the ground. Thanks to the blocks, the floor level was a foot or so above where I was standing, and there were no steps.

There was no answer to my knock.

I knocked again, waited again for an answer that didn't come.

Just for fun, I tried the doorknob. It turned easily, and I pushed on the door. It swung inward.

"Anybody home?" I yelled.

Still no answer. I looked around the dim room. There were two chairs, an old TV set with rabbit ears sitting on top, and an old coffee table. No rug on the floor. No pictures on the walls.

"Hello in there," I said, and stepped up into the room, letting the screen door swing shut behind me.

That was as far as I intended to go. I had a feeling that something was wrong here, and I didn't want any part of it.

Then I felt something brush against my leg. I must have been wound a little tighter than I thought, since I jumped straight up about a foot.

It was the cat, which had apparently heard me calling, come back around front, and followed me through the door.

"You sneaky son of a bitch," I said.

The cat paid me no attention at all, just stood there looking through the doorway into the next room, the hair on his back slowly rising.

My heartbeat was already accelerated, thanks to the cat's brushing my leg, and seeing the way he was behaving didn't do anything to calm me. He gave a low growl and moved back toward the screen.

I took a step backward too. If the cat didn't want to see more, I was pretty sure I didn't, either. I should have looked where I was stepping, though. I put my heel right on the cat's front paw, and he howled with fear and anger, a piercing shriek that I was pretty sure scared me a lot more than I had scared him.

He ran under one of the chairs and crouched down, while I stood still and tried to regulate my breathing. It was a good thing I hadn't brought my pistol, or by now the room would have been full of holes. I might even have shot the cat.

If there was anyone within a few blocks of the place, they would have showed themselves by now, or at least said something. The cat was loud enough to wake up a rock, and I might even have yelled myself while I was jumping.

So it wouldn't hurt to have a look in the next room.

Except that I didn't want to do it. A little of the cat's fear was in me now, and for the same reason. I could smell a little of what the cat smelled, and it didn't smell good. It smelled too much like the gator, too much like blood and corruption.

I looked anyway.

There were actually two doorways, one leading to a kitchen and one into a bedroom. The bedroom was where I looked.

That's where the dead woman was. She was wearing a dress that seemed obviously homemade and about two sizes too big. It was some kind of blue material, but it was stained red in the front by the blood. There was a small pool of blood beneath her. Most of it had soaked into the floor, staining it black. She looked frail and helpless in death.

The man was much bigger, and even dead he looked threatening. Big as a bear, Fred had told me, and that was a pretty apt description of Zach Holt. His face was as big and round as a dinner plate and covered with a thick black beard. He had on a flannel shirt with the sleeves rolled up and jeans faded almost white and covered with dirt and grass and other stains I couldn't identify and didn't care to.

There was more blood on him than on the woman, as if he'd been shot more times, and the cover was off the bed where he'd grabbed it in his huge hand and pulled it, as if in an attempt to pull himself up off the floor.

I looked around the rest of the room. Besides the bed, there was a chest of drawers that looked a hundred years old but which was probably a lot newer than that. It had just been beaten up a lot, maybe bought at a secondhand store. There was a closed door that I assumed led to a closet, and that was all. The Holts hadn't gone in for fancy living.

I went into the kitchen where the phone was and called Fred. "Call the sheriff," I said after I told him what I'd found. "And have somebody send an ambulance. Or a hearse."

I looked through the doorway into the front room and saw the cat, crouching under the chair and staring at me.

Deputy Norm Jackson was the first to arrive. He didn't say much, just looked at the bodies and confirmed my suspicion that they were the Holts. It was his opinion that we had best wait for the sheriff himself.

"We don't get much murder around here," he said. "Sheriff'll want to handle this himself."

Sheriff Tal Tolliver was a tall, rawboned man who looked good in his western-cut clothes. Better yet, he had a streak of pure white that ran down the right side of his hair. He wore boots with sharp-pointed toes. He looked more like a sheriff than anyone I'd ever seen.

Norm Jackson explained to him what I was doing there and how I'd found the bodies.

"A big-city private eye, huh?" Tolliver said, looking me over. "I don't believe I've ever seen one of those, except on TV—I like to watch that *Jake and the Fatman* whenever I get a chance." He had a deep, resonant voice that would make him a hit at any campaign speech. "You carry a pistol, son?"

He wasn't more than forty-five years old, which meant that if I was his son he was extremely precocious. I didn't mention that fact to him, however. I just said, "No, I don't."

"Good, good," he said. "We don't like folks coming into the county and carrying guns and killing folks. You just have a seat and wait here a while."

I sat in one of the chairs, the one the cat had been under. I had let him out before Jackson came.

Tolliver and Jackson went into the bedroom with their Polaroid camera and their evidence bags to perform their crime-scene investigation. I doubted they'd learn any more than I had.

The ambulance arrived while they were in there, and I pointed the way for two young men who didn't look especially eager to do their jobs.

The justice of the peace came in right behind them, and all in all it took about an hour to get things squared away.

When everyone but the law was gone, Tolliver came out of the bedroom. "I don't mind if you look for whoever it was that killed the gator on Fred Benton's place," he said. "But I hope you don't intend to get yourself mixed up in any of our other little problems around here."

"I hope not," I said. "Although I guess your deputy told you that someone took a shot at me and Fred today."

"Probably just some out-of-season hunter, didn't want

you to get too close to him and see who it was. This here is
a little bit different."

I couldn't argue with that. "Don't worry. All I wanted to
do was ask Zach Holt if he killed Fred's alligator."

"If he was the one, he's been punished enough for it,
wouldn't you say?" The sheriff smiled.

"Absolutely," I said.

"And you don't carry a gun, so you weren't the one who
punished him. You did say you don't carry a gun?"

I thought it might be a good idea to offer a small clarifi-
cation. "I meant that I wasn't carrying one now. I've used
one in the past, but I didn't think I'd need one to investigate
a dead alligator."

"Oh," he said. "Well, we'll want you to hold yourself available for questioning in this investigation."

"Am I a suspect?"

"You were in the house with 'em. You might've thought
Holt was the one who took a shot at you earlier."

"They looked like they'd been dead for a while," I said. I
didn't know why I was pushing it. I knew it wouldn't get me
anywhere.

"You could have killed them earlier, then come back. Re-
turning to the scene of the crime, like they say."

"I'll be available," I said.

I didn't want to argue anymore; I just wanted to get out
of the house. After all, he'd never come right out and said I
was a suspect. I couldn't blame him for wondering about me.
I was a stranger, and I was in the middle of a murder, for
whatever reason. It was a place he didn't like for me to be,
any more than I liked being there.

I went out into the yard. The sheriff's car was there, along
with the deputy's. The ambulance was still there as well. It
was dark now, and the light bar on the ambulance threw
dancing shadows around the place.

I was standing by my car, thinking about leaving, when
Deputy Jackson's bony hand landed on my shoulder. I turned
to face him.

"I guess you know I don't like you much, Smith," he said.

The feeling was mutual, but I wasn't going to be the one to tell him.

"I told you that I'd really hate to have a murder case on my hands," he went on, "and now I've got one. You told me you wouldn't bother anyone that didn't bother you first, but now there's a dead man and woman in that ambulance, and you're standin' here in their yard. I really don't like you, Smith."

I decided that it was time to speak up for myself. "I haven't bothered anyone, and I certainly didn't kill anyone."

I looked at the dark bulk of the house. Killing people wasn't in my line, whether Jackson knew it or not, and I was actually a little queasy just thinking about the two bodies.

"I think the sheriff believes that you're just an innocent bystander, lookin' for a gator killer," Jackson said. "Me, I'm not so sure. I'll be watching you, Smith. I'll be watching you real close. You won't want to make a wrong move."

He turned and walked back toward the house. I watched him go, his thin body looking like nothing more than a shadow of itself as the light flickered over it. I was beginning to wonder exactly what I'd gotten myself into.

Fred was curious, naturally, so I told him as much as I knew.

"You think this fits in with what-all else is goin' on around here?" he said.

"I don't have any idea," I said. "Do you usually have this much excitement?"

"You're kinda jokin' with me again, ain't you," he said. "A dead gator wouldn't be such a big deal, but murder? I don't know how long it's been since there was a murder in this county. And when you add in those shots somebody took at us today, well, you got enough excitement to last this place about ten years."

That's what I'd been afraid he would say. It was probably all tied in together, all right. Nothing else made any sense.

Maybe I could get a handle on it in the morning. Right now, I needed to make a phone call.

Fred said it would be all right to call Galveston. "Just don't talk too long."

Dino was irritated that I'd found it necessary to call. "Of course I fed the damn cat," he said. "You think I'd forget a thing like that?"

"Not really," I said. "Just checking."

"Trust me," Dino said. "Put that cat right out of your mind."

I told him I'd try.

$\triangledown$

7

THINGS DIDN'T GET any better the next day.

Fred woke me up early, and I hadn't slept too well. I dreamed all night that I was trying to get somewhere, walking along a sandy country road, looking for Jan, but I could never get to wherever it was that I was going. I didn't find Jan, either. I hadn't run in two days, but my legs felt as heavy and tired as if I'd just finished the Boston Marathon.

Fred hadn't gotten me up for breakfast, either. "There's somebody here you need to talk to," he said.

So I went into the bathroom and brushed my teeth and tried to make myself presentable in the few minutes he allowed me. The whole time I was getting dressed, he stood by the bed and tapped his foot on the floor.

He led me to the den, and this time instead of a deputy sheriff there were three people sitting on the couch. Two of them, a man and a woman, looked about Fred's age, but they hadn't aged quite as well. Their faces were lined and leathery, their eyes tired. They wore faded clothes that had been washed and dried in the sun a lot of times. They twisted their hands nervously when I walked through the door.

Beside them there was a woman who was much younger, probably ten years younger than me. She had long, straight blond hair and blue eyes. She'd spent a lot of time outdoors; her face was a smooth, even tan. She was as nervous as the other two, but she didn't show it by any movement. She showed it by sitting rock still, and by the shadow in her blue eyes.

I wished I'd shaved.

"These are the Stones," Fred said. "This here's Don."

The old man got off the couch and offered me his hand. It was rough from outdoor work, and he had a solid grip. He was at least five inches shorter than I was.

"That's his wife, Sue, and his daughter-in-law, Brenda."

Sue and Brenda looked at me from where they sat. A lot of the people in this area hadn't gotten to the stage where women shook hands with men. I nodded in their direction.

"Pleased to meet you," I said.

"Don's got a problem," Fred said.

I'd worked that out for myself. I just didn't know what the problem was.

"They've got my boy," the man said.

I looked at Fred.

"The sheriff," he said. "They arrested Perry last night."

"They say he killed Zach Holt, but he never done it," Don Stone said.

"Let's sit down and get this sorted out," Fred said.

I thought that was a good idea, and I suppose the others did too. Don went back to the couch while I took the chair I'd sat in the day before. Fred stood where he was.

"Perry and Zach have had a little trouble in the past," Fred said. "Mostly over poaching and such."

"We own a little land, 'bout a hundred acres," Don Stone said. "Not much, but we got a little lake on it, has a few gators in it. That Holt fella, we think he took one not long ago. Perry braced him about it, and they got into a little argument."

"A fight is what they got into," Fred said.

"A scuffle," Stone said. "That's all it was, just a little bit of a scuffle, with some pushin' and hard words."

"Not the way I heard it," Fred said.

"That's the way it was, though. Maybe there was a bruise or two, but nobody got hurt. Just a scuffle."

I should have felt relieved, in a way. After all, just last evening I had been afraid that Jackson was going to try pinning the murders on me. Now it looked as if he'd found someone more readily at hand, and someone with a more obvious motive.

"Even if it was just a scuffle," I said, "it sounds as if the word got around about it."

"I expect that ever'body around here knew," Fred said. "It's hard to keep a secret about a good fight."

"Scuffle," Stone said.

"Scuffle, then. You can call it whatever you want to, but you know good and well that people talked about it."

"Where did this . . . scuffle take place?" I said.

"Hurley Eckles's store," Stone told me.

A good place for it. Hurley was the type who'd tell everyone who stopped in about the fight that had happened right there at his place of business.

"Even with something like that, though, the sheriff would need something else," I said. "He wouldn't arrest someone just because he had a fight with Holt. There must be more to it than that."

Nobody said anything.

"It's sure gotten quiet all of a sudden," I said after about half a minute had gone by.

"That's because there's not anything else," Stone said. "They just up and arrested Perry for that one reason. There's not anything else."

I didn't believe him, but I didn't press it. "So what does all that have to do with me?"

"Word gets around," Fred said. "Just like word got around about the fight. The Stones heard I'd hired somebody to look into the gator killin', and they heard you were the one that found the bodies yesterday, so they thought. . . ."

"We thought you might be able to help us," Brenda Stone said.

I had been wondering if she could speak. Now I knew. Her voice was soft and husky, the kind of voice that made me want to hear more of it.

"I'm not sure I can," I said. "I've been hired already, and I usually don't take but one client at a time. The sheriff's deputy has warned me to keep out of this case." He hadn't, not exactly, but I knew that Jackson wouldn't welcome my poking around in things, not after what he'd said to me.

"It's all the same case," Fred said. "You and I've already decided that. You don't have to do anything you wouldn't have done in the first place. If it ties in, it's not your fault."

I wasn't sure Jackson would see it that way, but I said, "All right, I'll see what I can do. As long as it fits in with the job I've already got."

"That's fine. That's all we could ask for," Stone said, rising.

The two women stood up as well.

"We surely do thank you, Mr. Benton," Stone said, taking Fred's hand. "We surely do."

"Thank you, too, Mr. Smith," the younger Mrs. Stone said as they were ushered out of the room.

I watched them go, Fred showing them to the door. Then I went into the kitchen to see if there was any breakfast.

Mary was standing at the stove. "Bacon and eggs?" she said.

"Sounds good to me."

She tossed strips of bacon into a heavy black iron skillet.

When they started to sizzle, I said, "Mary, how do you feel about this place?"

She glanced at me, then back at the bacon. "How do you mean?"

"I mean, do you feel the same way Fred does? About the gators and things? Or would you rather see this place developed and turned into parkland?"

Mary reached into the skillet with a fork and turned the bacon. It smelled even better than it had the day before.

"Whatever Fred wants is fine with me," Mary said. "This land has been in my family for a while, but I'm not attached to it. It's just land. Fred's the one who cares about it, and all the critters on it. I've never been that interested in what he does with it. It keeps him happy, and that's all that matters to me."

She took the bacon out and laid it on a paper towel to drain, then cracked an egg on the edge of the skillet. She broke the shell in half and dropped the egg into the bacon grease.

"One or two?" she said.

"Two," I said, wondering what my cholesterol level would be by the time I finished this job.

She broke another egg into the skillet and stirred them around with the fork. "Fred is all I'm really interested in, you see. We've been together for a long time, and I like to see him busy and happy. As far as I'm concerned, this land is his. There's never been any dispute between us about that. If he wants to find out who killed that alligator, then I hope you do it."

She dumped the eggs on a plate and put the bacon on with them. "I'll get you some toast," she said.

While I was eating, Fred came back in. "I thought you ought to meet those people," he said. "They're pretty nice folks, and Perry wouldn't kill anybody."

I hadn't met Perry, but I was willing to dispute that statement. You never could tell who might kill someone.

"Have you known them long?" I asked.

"More than thirty years. Since before Perry was born. They aren't like some families around here. They work hard, keep to themselves, and don't bother other people."

"Except when they get into scuffles," I said, pushing away the empty plate.

"That's the exception, all right. Perry got a little hot under the collar about that missing gator. It's understandable."

Understandable if you were Fred Benton, at least. No wonder he was taking up for Perry. They seemed to have similar interests.

"There's more to the story than anyone was telling, though," I said. "Do you know it?"

Fred looked sheepish. "I've heard stories."

"What are they?"

"I don't like to repeat that stuff," he said, looking at Mary.

Mary laughed. "I'm a grown woman, and I've heard the rumors too. It won't scandalize me to hear them again."

"Well," Fred said to me, "I guess you have to know. There's been talk that Zach Holt and Brenda Stone . . . uh . . . fooled around some."

"For goodness' sakes, Fred," Mary said, "don't be so shy."

Fred shrugged. "Brenda and Zach went out some in high school. That was nearly fifteen years ago, though, and it all ended when Zach dropped out. He didn't take too well to formal education, but he was a helluva football player. We all hated it when he dropped out, but he was wild even then, huntin' gators for skins just like he does now. Did, I mean. I guess he won't be doin' much of that anymore."

"He won't be doing much of anything," I said. "Somebody cured him of the habit."

I found myself wondering where Fred had been when Holt was killed. I wondered, for that matter, when he *was* killed. I'm no expert in those things, but I would have guessed that he hadn't been dead long.

I also wondered what kind of gun had been used to kill him and his wife, whether it had been a rifle or a pistol. I guessed a pistol. It didn't seem likely that you'd let someone in your house if he was carrying a rifle, though in Texas you never knew.

And that reminded me of something that I needed to do.

"Fred," I said, "I hate to do this so soon after that fine breakfast, but it's time for us to look at that alligator again."

*   *   *

The smell was even worse, and I could hear the buzzing of the flies from farther away. The thought of what we were about to do made the bile rise in my throat.

I must have looked pretty green. Fred said, "You sure you got the stomach for this?"

"No," I said. "But I'll give it a try. Unless you want to do it."

He shook his head. "I'll pass. You're the high-salaried detective." He got a Camel out of his pack and lit up.

"Jackson should have done this himself," I said. "I'm beginning to wonder about him."

Fred took a deep drag on the Camel. "I don't much blame him for not doin' it. That smell—"

"It's his job, though," I said. I thought about that. "Mine, too, I guess, since you hired me. Where're those gloves?"

"Right here."

He handed me a pair of Playtex rubber gloves, bright yellow, that he had taken from under the sink at his house. I pulled them on, stretching them considerably in the process.

"You think your wife will want these back?"

"I doubt that very seriously. You don't have to be careful with 'em."

"How about the mask?"

He handed me an allergy mask. I put the elastic band in back of my head and pulled the mask over my nose and mouth.

"You look more like a doctor in that thing than I do when I'm wearing one," he said. " 'Course when I'm wearing it, I'm usually ridin' a lawn mower."

"Scalpel," I said, putting out my right hand, palm up.

He handed me a butcher knife that he had taken from Mary's knife drawer. I was sure she'd want it back. Maybe Fred would clean it.

I walked over to the rotting gator. "Why hasn't one of his buddies hauled him into the water and eaten him?" I said, my voice distorted only slightly by the mask, which wasn't really doing much to help with the smell.

"I don't know," Fred said. "Usually they'll eat just about

anything, and that's a fact. They generally like to put things up and let 'em rot under water where they don't stink so bad, but I don't think the smell would put them off like it does me and you. Or maybe it's just me."

"It's not just you," I said. I didn't want to do what I was about to do, but I couldn't think of any way to put it off any longer.

I looked at the carcass, trying to see where the bullets had hit it. I spotted a likely looking place where a large hunk of flesh had been gouged out and decided to start there. I smacked the carcass with the flat of the knife blade a couple of times, hard. Flies rose up in a buzzing cloud, and I got down to work.

I dug around in the decaying meat, trying to avoid contact with it as much as possible. It wasn't easy. The gloves didn't come up much farther than my wrists, and I brushed against the body several times with my shirt and pants. Parts of it stuck to me where I touched it.

I found a bullet, though, partially embedded in a bone of one kind or another. My knowledge of alligator skeletal structure is sketchy at best.

I popped the bullet out of the bone with the knife blade and held it in my gloved hand. It was in pretty good shape, considering. Hardly flattened at all. I was glad, because I didn't feel like digging for another one. The heat, the smell, the feel of the tough meat, the flies swarming around my head, were all too much.

I handed the bullet to Fred. "Excuse me," I said. I walked over to a tree, took off the mask, and threw up.

Fred politely refrained from comment. I like to think he would have felt the same way I did had he done the job.

I walked back to the Jeep. "Shouldn't have eaten such a big breakfast," I said. "Let's get out of here."

Fred cranked up and we took off. "What're you gonna do with this bullet now that we got it?" he said.

"Where is it?" I said, trying to peel off the gloves without getting anything on my hands.

"In my pocket."

"That's a good place for it right now." I tossed the gloves behind me into the Jeep. "It might come in handy later. We need a gun to match it up with."

"Rifle," he said.

"Right."

I was pretty sure the county didn't have facilities to do a ballistics test, but there was no doubt that the Houston police did. I didn't know how good those facilities were, however. I wondered if the ballistics people had ever gotten that water tank to fire into. They had been wanting one for years but had been forced to make do with more primitive methods, thanks to a lack of funds.

"You think you could find out what kind of weapon killed Zach Holt and his wife?" I said as we bounced across the open ranch land.

"Maybe. I could ask. I know the doctor they use for autopsies. He might tell me quicker than the sheriff."

"Good idea. I'll bet it wasn't a rifle, but it wouldn't hurt to be sure."

"I'll see what I can do," he said, swerving to miss a small log.

My stomach lurched, but I didn't disgrace myself.

When we got back to the house, I changed clothes. I seemed to be doing a lot of that lately. This was turning out to be a messy case both literally and figuratively.

Then I looked for Fred and found him outside, hosing down the knife and the gloves.

"I think these'll clean up just fine," he said.

"I won't tell if you won't."

"That's a deal, then." He handed me the hose and walked over to turn off the water.

"Tell me something, Fred," I said.

"What's that?"

"There's more to this Brenda Stone and Zach Holt thing, isn't there?"

He sighed. "Yeah," he said. "I guess there is, at that."

▽

8

THE STORY WAS simple enough, and there really wasn't much more to it than Fred had already told me.

The rumor in town was that Zach and Brenda hadn't quite forgotten each other after high school, or else they'd suddenly remembered. Whichever way it was didn't matter, according to the talk, because they'd started seeing each other again. Not publicly, of course. But seeing each other nonetheless. And doing a good bit more than "fooling around."

"And supposedly Perry knows about it," Fred finished. That was the new bit of information I'd been looking for.

"If they weren't going out in public, how does anyone know what they were doing?" I said. It seemed like a logical question to me.

"I don't know," Fred said. "That's just the way it is around here. You just hear things. Like it's in the air. It's hard to keep a secret."

"Like the business of the state wanting to buy some land for a park."

"Like that. One day you don't hear anything at all, and the next day the story's all over town."

"You think there's anything to that one?"

"Which one?"

"The one about the park."

"Could be, but I doubt it. Something like that comes up ever' year or so. One time, it's that some big oil company's gonna come in here and lease all the acreage. The next time it's the state. I don't pay much attention anymore."

"You think I could get in to talk to Perry Stone?"

"You might. Depends on how the sheriff's feeling."

"I think I'll give it a try," I said. I didn't have any other bright ideas.

Except one.

"You better give me that bullet," I said.

Fred handed me the gray metal lump from his pocket. I was glad I'd dug it out of the gator instead of having someone dig it out of me.

"You got a use for it?" he said.

"I thought that if the sheriff and I got along real well, he might tell me about the rifles he found in Zach Holt's house. If he found any. You tell me Holt was a hunter, so there must have been some around."

"You see any?"

"No, but I wasn't exactly looking. Anyway, if there were any, and if this bullet was fired from one of them, then your case is solved."

"You planning to go home if you've got all that figured right?"

"I don't know," I said. It would be the smart thing to do, though. Go home and forget the rest of it, which didn't involve me at all.

"I'll pay for your time if you stay," he said.

"I wasn't thinking about the money," I said, feeling vaguely guilty that he even thought I might be.

"I didn't think you were, but I wanted to make sure."

I flipped the bullet up into the air, caught it, and stuck it in my jeans. "I may not find out anything. The deputy doesn't like me."

"Don't feel bad about that," Fred said. "He don't like any-body."

I got in the Subaru and went to jail.

The county seat was a small town, but the jail was new. It was just off the main road and had walls that looked like polished granite, two stories tall.

The inside was air-conditioned and cool. A young woman in uniform directed me to the sheriff's office, which was toward the back of a large room cluttered with desks and office chairs.

Tal Tolliver was looking at some papers on his desk when the woman tapped on the glass top of his open door. He looked up and saw us, not looking overly thrilled at the sight of me. He motioned me in.

"What can I do for you, Smith?" he said. He didn't bother to stand up or to shake my hand.

"I'd like to talk to Perry Stone," I said. "I'm representing his family."

"They hire you?"

"Something like that."

He let it pass. "Tell you he got railroaded? Tell you we got no evidence?" He seemed more belligerent than he had the night before.

"They didn't say."

"They may be right," he said.

"What?" I thought I must have heard him incorrectly. He couldn't have said what I thought he did.

But he had. "They may be right. I think Deppidy Jackson reacted a little fast on this one."

"They really didn't fill me in," I said, realizing that I was telling the truth.

"Well," he said, running his hand down the white streak in his hair, "there's been some talk around town about Holt and Perry's wife. You met her?"

I said that I had.

"Then you might understand. Zach's wife wasn't any

beauty, and he and Brenda Stone were a hot item a long time back. Maybe there's nothing to the rumors, or maybe there is, but that doesn't matter. Jackson went to Perry's house, just to ask him about things, you know, account for his whereabouts and so on. Perry got hot under the collar, took a swing at Jackson."

"He have a reputation for that?"

"Jackson?"

"Perry," I said. I was thinking about Perry's "scuffle" with Holt.

"I guess you could say that. He had a fight with Holt about some damn alligator not long ago."

"So Jackson brought him in."

"He sure did. He's tougher than he looks. Perry didn't have a chance. You can talk to him if you want to. I'm not sure we're even gonna hold him much longer."

He led me up to the second floor, where the cells were. They were very clean, and Perry Stone was sitting on his bunk, wearing a bright orange jumpsuit.

"Visitor," the sheriff said. He called the jailer over, and they let Stone out, taking us to a small visitors' room.

Tolliver and the jailer left, and I introduced myself to Stone and told him what I was doing there. He was a medium-sized man, about five nine, but solid. There was a bruise on the side of his face.

"Jackson give you that?" I said.

He rubbed the bruise lightly. "I guess I deserved it," he said. "I started things. He just finished them."

"You didn't like being accused of murder?"

"It wasn't that," he said. "I didn't like the things he was saying about my wife. About her and Holt."

"Are they true?"

His face got dark and his hands clenched. Then he slowly relaxed. "You say you're working for my family, but that shouldn't give you leave to talk to me like that."

"I just wondered how you felt about it," I said. "Now I know."

"I guess you do."

"So how do you feel about alligators?"

He looked puzzled. "Alligators?"

"That's right. Alligators."

"I like 'em all right. If you mean something about that scuffle I had with Zach Holt, well, that was my fault too. But I still think he killed that gator."

"Where were you when Holt was killed? Do you have an alibi?"

"I was right here in town most of the day, and plenty of people saw me. I don't know when he was killed, but I didn't do it anytime yesterday."

"There seem to be a lot of strange things happening around here lately," I said. "Zach Holt and his wife are murdered, someone kills one of Fred Benton's gators, you get in fights, there's rumors of a big land buy—"

"That's no rumor," he said. "I heard that for the truth. But you're right about a lot of things going on. Rustlin', too."

Fred had mentioned the rustling earlier, but I'd forgotten about it. "You had any cows stolen?" I said.

"Not me, but I've heard the trucks at night. Not on my road, or I'd've done something about it."

"What could you do?"

"Blow out a tire for 'em. I got a shotgun. I can protect what's mine."

Perry Stone was a hotheaded young man. I wondered if maybe the sheriff wasn't being a little soft-hearted in excusing him so lightly.

I told Perry that I'd do what I could to help him, but that he didn't really need my help. I said that I thought he'd be released soon.

"It's a good thing, too," he said. "They don't have any evidence on me."

I called for the jailer, who took Perry back to his cell while I went back downstairs. Sheriff Tolliver was still sitting at his desk, so I went in and gave him the bullet.

"Where'd this come from?" he said, rolling it around in his fingers.

I told him.

"Wonder why Jackson didn't think about that?"

Since I'd wondered the same thing, I just shook my head.

"Maybe he didn't think it was important," Tolliver said. "But we'll see what we can do. Zach Holt had a couple of rifles. We could have 'em checked."

"I'd appreciate that," I said.

"Well, I'll let you know," he said.

I could tell an exit line when I heard it, so I left.

Going back to Fred's house, I decided to take another drive around the countryside to get a little more familiar with the area. It's amazing sometimes how many little dirt and gravel roads there are in the rural parts of Texas, all of them leading somewhere, to a house or a pasture or a fishing hole or a place where one of those things used to be. It would be easy enough for someone who didn't know his way around to get lost, so I tried to keep up with my twistings and turnings.

I passed grazing cattle, giant oaks hung thickly with Spanish moss, rice fields, and houses long abandoned and half falling down. There were also houses that looked almost new, with satellite dishes in their front yards, boats under the carports, and lawns as fine as any in the city.

I drove past the Holt house and saw the gray cat sitting on top of the rusting car. I wondered what would happen to him and even thought briefly of trying to catch him so that I could take him to Galveston as a companion for Nameless. But only briefly. Nameless didn't seem the type to welcome companions. He didn't even like me that much, and I was the one who usually fed him.

Winding down near the river bottoms, I found the roads narrower, with the trees hanging their moss-heavy branches out over fences and over my head. The roads also got twistier and rougher, and I was beginning to wonder if I knew just exactly where I was. It was time to think about getting back to Fred's.

There were no houses at all around now, and there was no place for me to turn the car. The road was too narrow for a three-point turn, even in the Subaru, and I was afraid that any minute it would turn into a cow path or a rabbit trail.

Finally I came to a crossroads at a place where the fence posts seemed close enough to reach out and touch. I stopped the car to decide which way to turn, but when I looked to the left I saw the tail end of a gray car in the distance.

It was hard to tell, since the car was kicking up a trail of white dust, but it looked as if it might be the Oldsmobile I'd seen yesterday, the one with the flat tire. With everything else that had been happening, I'd completely forgotten about the car and its hard-looking driver Gene Ransome. I wondered what he was doing down in the woods. This didn't seem a very likely spot for him to be, even if he was a salesman.

I decided to follow him, for no better reason than the fact that he looked more like a cheap hood from a 1950s B-movie than a salesman, and turned the Subaru to the left.

I drove along behind him for about a mile, trying to keep him in sight around all the twists and turns of the narrow road. He wasn't in any hurry, so I didn't have any trouble. As we were coming up on a weather-beaten old house that listed to the right at about a forty-five-degree angle, he slowed down even more. Then he pulled in beside the house, concealing his car from me.

I didn't know whether to drive on by or to stop and wait. If he saw me pass, it wouldn't mean anything to him. He might not even recognize the car, though I doubted that he met many Subarus in this part of the country. If I waited, though, and he'd already spotted me, he'd wonder what was going on.

So I kept going.

When I got to the house, there was no car.

I'd expected it to be parked in the shade by the house, but it wasn't. I didn't see the car anywhere.

I backed up and turned into the yard, parking the Subaru in front of the house. The place was in terrible shape, rotten boards, no glass in the windows, most of the roof gone. I got out and walked to the porch, through thick weeds that grabbed at my jeans.

The porch was still there, but only barely. Most of the boards were missing, and weeds grew right up in front of the door. Wherever Gene Ransome had gone, I was sure he wasn't in the house.

So where was he, then? He had to be around somewhere.

I walked to the other side of the house. There were well-worn ruts in the ground, and I looked out behind the house. The ruts continued through the grass and weeds and into the trees.

Maybe there was something back in there, like a grocery store. Maybe Ransome was just a simple salesman, making his calls. Maybe there was a simple, logical explanation for his disappearance into the trees.

Maybe I could change myself into Captain Marvel by yelling "Shazam!"

I looked along the ruts, but they didn't tell me anything, except that a guy driving an Oldsmobile in a place like this was just begging for a flat tire.

The same went for a guy driving a Subaru, but I could always walk. Too bad I didn't know how far Ransome was going. I could start back in there and run across him in five minutes, or I could find a rutted track that went on for miles.

I wasn't going to find out anything by standing where I was, though, unless I simply waited for Ransome to come back and then followed him again, or waited and then went down the ruts to see what was there.

The latter idea appealed to me. I didn't know what Ransome was doing, legal or illegal, I didn't know whether he was armed if what he was doing *was* illegal, and I didn't have a gun of my own.

The only problem was my car. He'd see that for sure. I went back to the Subaru, apologized to my tires, and drove right across the open field to the trees. There was a sizable clump of bushes, and I drove right in.

I had to force the door open against the resisting branches, but I managed to get out and get back to the field with only minor scrapes and scratches. The Subaru's finish suffered more than I did, but a few more scratches here and there on its surface wouldn't even be noticed.

I walked back to the house and went inside to wait.

It wasn't entirely empty. There was the remains of a mattress, the ticking spotted with mold and the stuffing coming out. There were also some random pages from a magazine, most of them yellowing and gnawed by silverfish and other bugs.

I sat on the mattress, hoping that no ancient disease clung to it. It was comfortable enough, so I dragged it over by the window on the side where the car would pass. I lay down directly underneath the window and waited for the sound of the car.

▽

9

THE HOUSE WAS hot, and the humidity was just as bad inside as out, but it wasn't stuffy, what with all the window glass missing, and I must have fallen asleep. I was dreaming something about a storm in the Gulf, with Jan drowning and me struggling to get to her through the surf, when I woke up and realized that the noise in my dream wasn't the surf at all but the sound of a car engine.

I had the presence of mind not to sit up, though I'm usually not especially alert when I first come out of sleep. The car passed by the window as I lay there.

I tiptoed across the rotten, slanted floor as if there might be someone to hear me and looked around the side of a door. Ransome's car turned in the direction he'd been heading before, and he drove away.

I went out and started down the ruts. It was midafternoon now, and there was a slight breeze out of the south. I imagined I could smell the refineries and chemical plants from down on the coast.

I wasn't quite to the trees when I heard another noise. I stopped where I was and listened. It sounded like another car coming from the woods. I hadn't thought that Ransome

might be meeting someone. I hadn't thought there was anyone there to meet.

What the hell, maybe there really *was* a grocery store back
there.

And even if there wasn't, there was really no place for me
to go. It was too far back to the house, and the weeds weren't
really high enough to hide me.

Suddenly the sound got louder. I peered into the trees, but
I didn't see anything.

Standing out where I was in the sunlight, I was easy to
see from back in the trees, though, and someone must have
seen me.

I recognized the next sounds. Someone was gunning an
engine, winding it up, and then letting off the clutch so that
the tires spun on the hard caliche soil. There was a crackling
and popping, as if some rotten tree branches were being run
over and crushed. Then the vehicle exploded out of the trees
and came straight at me.

It was one of those jacked-up four-by-four trucks with
reinforced springs and pumped-up shocks that raised it so
high you practically needed a stepladder to get up into the
cab. The tires were huge spinning rings of heavily treaded
rubber that looked as big as tractor tires and were moving
much faster than most tractors ever traveled.

The silver bars of the truck's grille grinned at me like the
teeth of some gigantic alligator from Fred's lake, and the
bumper looked as high as my head. I could imagine my skull
splitting like a rotten watermelon when it hit me, my teeth
being mashed to the back of my neck.

I didn't stand around waiting for that to happen, though. I
threw myself to the side and rolled through the grass and weeds.

Then I was up and running, praying that my bum knee
wouldn't give way and throw me to the ground.

The driver of the truck made a magnificent skidding turn
that I would have thought might be extremely dangerous to
him. In fact, I was hoping that the truck would turn right
over on top of itself, thanks to the high tires.

It didn't happen. The tires gouged huge chunks of grass and dirt up and threw them into the air behind the truck as the driver changed course and came after me, moving his vehicle along a lot faster than I was capable of moving myself.

My knee was starting to twinge, but there was nothing I could do but run.

If I had been calmer, say if I had been watching the scene in a movie, I might have thought of things like getting the license number of the truck or of getting a look at the driver.

And I did think of those things, even in my situation, but only vaguely. Even in less stressful circumstances, doing either one would have been next to impossible.

For one thing, there was no front license plate.

For another, the windows were so heavily darkened that there was no way to see inside. Even the windshield was darker than normal.

All I could really see was that the truck was black and that the silver letters F O R D were stretched across the front of the hood.

Meanwhile, I was running as fast as I could across the field toward the ramshackle house, stepping in holes, stumbling over hillocks, tripping on vines, and cursing myself for ever getting into this mess in the first place.

The truck was right behind me, bouncing along as if it were on some kind of crazy trampoline, not bothered at all by the things that were giving me such grief.

I was pretty sure I was going to make it to the house, however, and I thought that if I could get inside, I would be safe.

It was a close race, but I won it, throwing myself into the house through an open window and scrapping across the floor on my hands and knees before rolling over and bumping into a wall.

I lay there trying to catch my breath and noticing that my bad knee felt something like a piece of steak that had just been put through the grinder. At least it had held up, though

I knew that if I had taken many more steps, it would have collapsed and I would have been mashed like a June bug under the truck's gigantic tires.

I got my breath back soon enough. All the jogging I do is good for that, if for nothing else, and maybe it had even strengthened the knee. For a second I wished I was down on the Galveston seawall, doing my daily run and looking at the women in their microscopic bathing suits as the season drew on toward fall.

The sound of the truck brought me back to where I was. The driver was revving up the engine again, and I could hear the dirt flying from under the wheels and striking the metal wheel coverings.

Surely he wasn't crazy enough to—

He was.

I got a quick glimpse of the truck through the window I had just entered before the driver rammed the house.

It would be nice to say that the house exploded like a building made of matchsticks, but that wouldn't be true.

That's exactly what I thought would happen, given the condition of the house, but it was more solid than it appeared to be.

There was a rending and tearing, accompanied by the sound of very old and very rusty nails being pulled from the boards where they had been embedded for years, and then the wall opposite of where I was sitting bulged inward alarmingly. But everything held together.

The truck backed up.

Whoever was driving it had to be crazy. He was going to give it another try.

Well, that was his privilege, but I wasn't going to be there when he did it.

I slithered on the floor into the other room, trying to keep below the level of the windows, and slid out onto the porch, which was slanting even more than it had earlier.

I was rolling off the porch when the truck hit again, and I stumbled through the dust far enough to avoid the porch supports as they toppled. The roof slid off and crackled into a heap just before the walls fell over on it.

I was choking in the dust and hoping that the driver of the truck wouldn't be able to see me rubber-legging it toward the Subaru.

He did see me, though.

I heard him coming and stumbled forward, trying to ignore the pain in my knee, which was making me list dangerously to the right. There was no way I could get to the car before he flattened me.

I wished I had an elephant rifle, and for a fleeting second I imagined myself turning to face the truck, leveling my large-bore rifle on the stunned driver's vehicle, and sending two or three shots through his engine block.

It was a fine fantasy, but in reality I didn't have the tools. I didn't even have a pea shooter.

The truck was nearly upon me. It was time to do something really stupid.

I stopped, turned, and faced the truck, trying to clear my eyes with the back of my hand.

He was coming at me, and he was coming fast.

I charged him.

I'd thought he might be so surprised that he might stop, but of course that didn't happen.

He was surprised enough, however, that he at least took his foot off the accelerator and slowed down a bit.

I didn't. I kept right on going.

He pressed the accelerator again, but by then I was very close. I hoped that I was so close he couldn't see me over the hood.

I threw myself forward and lay flat, my face pressed into the dirt.

He sailed right over me.

I knew he wouldn't be fooled for long, if he was fooled at all. There had been no impact, and he would realize that very soon, but I was up and following him as fast as I could.

The brake lights came on, but I was almost close enough

to touch the back bumper. There was a license plate whose number I couldn't read. It was smeared with mud.

If only he didn't back up.

Turn, I thought at him. *Turn, you bastard.*

He did, and I followed the bumper, trying to reach out and grab the ball of the trailer hitch I saw there.

I couldn't reach it, but as he swung the rear end around, I followed. When he started forward toward the place where he thought I might be lying, I ran on toward the Subaru in the bushes.

He would be looking for me in the field, and his gaze would be occupied for a few seconds.

That was the theory.

And while he was looking for me where I wasn't, I would be getting the Subaru out of the bushes and making my getaway.

The problem with that idea was of course that the truck would mash the Subaru flatter than a steamrollered pancake.

Well, that wasn't true, but it certainly wouldn't be an even matchup.

I got to the Subaru with the side of my knee throbbing and swelling. I could almost see the skin splitting open and the kneecap spilling out and landing on the ground beside me. Obviously I was getting hysterical.

I forced the car door open against the brush and squeezed in. The Subaru started immediately, just as always, and I backed into the field.

The black truck was already on the job, rolling after me. I suddenly recalled a picture I'd seen in a book when I was a kid, a book about dinosaurs. The picture was of tyrannosaurus rex pursuing its hapless prey, some smaller, birdlike creature. I wondered what a photograph of the truck and the Subaru would look like to someone a few million years from now, but I was bounding around inside the car too much to worry about it. It was all I could do to keep my hands on the wheel and my foot on the accelerator.

It was obvious that I wasn't going to be able to escape, not by a long shot, so once more I decided that I'd have to do something that the driver didn't expect.

I couldn't charge him again; small as the Subaru was, it wouldn't quite make it under the truck's bumper.

So I turned and drove into the woods.

What I hoped was that I could avoid clumps of brush big enough to stop the car but find my way between some trees that were growing so close together that whoever was following me in the truck wouldn't be able to follow.

If I could avoid a puncture to any of my tires, I might make it out alive. It wasn't a great plan, but it was all I could come up with. It was better than getting plowed under by truckosaurus.

The opening I found and drove into was small, but not small enough. The Ford was crashing along behind me like a drunken rhino, and I looked for another turn while trying to avoid trees whose branches whipped across my windshield and whacked against my headlights.

I wanted to get back to the field somehow and then back onto the road. I was afraid that if I got too deep into the trees I might get lost and never find my way out. I didn't have a merit badge in woodcraft.

It was like a nightmare, weaving around among the trees and trying not to hit any of them, sort of like being lost in an enchanted forest in a Disney movie, with trees that have arms and faces and that reach out for you as they twist and writhe. I was never going to curse about driving on the Gulf Freeway at rush hour again. Even that was better than those trees.

And my car would never be the same. The old paint was being raked off in record amounts by the scratching of the tree branches, and I could only guess what might be happening to the undercarriage.

Somehow I managed to get turned around, ding enough openings, and get back to the field. I came out near the ruts that Ransome had been on, the very ruts I'd started to investigate only a few minutes before, though it seemed like hours now.

I realized that I could no longer hear the truck behind me, and I gave the car all the gas I could. It shuddered down the ruts a little faster, and I turned onto the county road and headed in the direction I hoped would lead me to Fred's house.

I liked to think that the truck was stuck back there in the woods with a tree trunk through its radiator grille. I wasn't going back to look for it, though. Not even on a bet.

"Sounds like you've had an interestin' day, all right," Fred said when I'd filled him in on the events in the jail and afterward. "You think Tolliver can do anything with that bullet?"

"Not unless we get one to match it," I said.

It was only about thirty minutes later, and I was sitting in Fred's kitchen, drinking a Big Red and wondering if we hadn't had this conversation before. I was also wondering why my good knee still felt like jelly and why my thighs seemed weak and trembly. I didn't have to wonder why my bad knee was throbbing; I knew the answer to that one.

"Where exactly was this place where you found the road to the woods?" Fred said. He was smoking a Camel and drinking lemonade from a glass beaded with drops of water.

I tried to tell him.

"Sounds a little like the old Overton place. Not too far from here," he said.

"It's not too far, that's for sure. I would've been back sooner if I hadn't made a wrong turn or two."

"Ought to be easy to find, that old house fallin' down and all." He took a drink of lemonade and tapped his cigarette into the sink.

"Mary'd give me hell if she saw that," he said. He turned on the tap and washed the ashes down the drain. "I bet that old house is a sight to see."

It finally dawned on me what he was trying to suggest.

"You want to go back there and look around?" I said.

"I wouldn't be goin' back. I ain't been there yet."

"Well, I have, and I'm not so sure I want to go back."

"You won't be able to find what's at the end of that road if you don't," he said.

It was hard to argue with that, but I wasn't sure that whatever was at the end of the road was any of my business. I said as much to Fred.

"You might be right, at that," he said. "Only thing is, and this is what interests me, some of my land joins the Overton place back down in there. There's some real swampy land in those river bottoms, places I don't hardly ever get to. I'd like to know what's goin' on back in there if I could find out."

"You think there's some connection to the dead gator?"

"Can't ever tell." He took the butt of the Camel, turned on the tap, and ran water over it. Then he tossed the butt in the trash. " 'Less you go look, that is."

"First the phone calls, then the noises, then the dead gator," I said. "Then the dead people."

"How about Perry Stone? You think he did it?"

"Did what? All of the above?"

"Let's just say killin' the people."

"No," I said. "I don't think he did that or any of the other things, and I wonder why Jackson was in such a hurry to arrest him. Stone told me he had plenty of witnesses to say he was in town all day on the day Holt was shot."

"Murder's kind of rare around here," Fred said. "Maybe they were just in a hurry to make an arrest."

I drank the last of the Big Red. "Maybe so. But that Jackson bothers me. Stone was bruised up."

I gave Fred the throwaway bottle, and he put it in the trash with his cigarette butt. "Jackson's a little mean. That's not very unusual around here."

"Then there's the matter of that bullet in the alligator. The one he didn't look for," I said. "He looked for the brass, though."

"You like diggin' in that gator?" Fred said.

"Not much," I said.

"Well?"

"I guess you're right," I said. But I still wondered.

"And what about this Gene Ransome?" I said. "You ever heard of him? Ever seen him around?"

"Nope."

"Well, he knows you. And he knows Hurley Eckles."

Then I thought about that. Ransome had *said* that he knew Eckles and Fred. That didn't mean he was telling the truth. This was getting more complicated by the minute.

"Hurley knows lots of folks," Fred said. "You could ask him. You could ask him about that big black Ford truck, too, but I bet there's more of them around than you'd think."

He was probably right, but there couldn't be more than two or three of them. I didn't think Eckles would tell me anything, though. He didn't like me very much.

"Well, we gonna check out that road in the woods or not?" Fred said.

"I guess so," I said.

I was beginning to wish that I was at home with my cat and a good book. I hoped Dino would feed Nameless, but I wasn't going to call and ask again. I needed all the friends I could get.

▽

10

WE DIDN'T GO straight there, however.

I talked Fred into going by Hurley Eckles's place, just in case the Ford truck had turned up there.

"Hurley didn't own a truck like that," Fred said. "I'd know about it if he did."

"What about his buddy?" I said.

"Which one is that?"

"Temp," I said. "Or something like that. Doesn't have much to say."

"Tall, skinny fella?"

"That's the one."

"Temp Stansell. He and Hurley talk and spit a lot, but Hurley does most of the talkin'."

They were still sitting where I'd seen them the day before. Or they were sitting there again. I assumed that surely they'd moved at one time or another. It was hard to tell, though.

We parked the Jeep and got out. I was going to take the direct approach this time, but Hurley beat me to the punch.

"You still lookin' to buy some land around here?" he said, spitting snuff on the ground.

Fred looked at him and started to say something, but I cut

in. I didn't want Hurley calling him a horse turd to his face
and cause a fight. Hurley was younger and heavier, but I
thought Fred had a pretty good chance against him if it came
to that. I just didn't want to be the cause of it.

"I'm investigating a crime," I said. "I'm sorry about trying
to mislead you earlier, but I was afraid you might not coop-
erate if I told you what I was really looking for."

He chuckled, a wet, unpleasant sound, filtered as it was
through the snuff in his mouth. "You sure got a long way by
lyin', didn't you?" he said.

Temp shook beside him with silent laughter. It didn't take
much to get a laugh from those two, but then they didn't
often have the opportunity to make fun of someone like me.

"I apologize," I said.

"Yeah, I heard you. So is that why you came back? To tell
me and Temp how sorry you was?"

"Not exactly," I said. "I wanted to ask you about something else."

Hurley looked at Fred and spit in the direction of his shoe.
"I didn't kill no gator," he said.

Fred didn't say anything. We'd agreed on the way over that
he'd keep out of things, thanks to his mutual antagonism
with Hurley. I could see that he was having a hard time
controlling himself, however. The back of his neck was getting red.

"It's not about a gator," I said.

"I didn't kill neither of them Holts," Hurley said. "They
was good customers."

Temp shook his head sadly. It was tough to lose good
customers.

"That's not it either," I said.

For a second he looked puzzled, like a frog surprised by a
sudden light. He took off his shabby old hat and fanned it
in front of his face.

I didn't say anything.

After a few seconds of fanning, he said, "Well, what is it
then?" He put the hat back on.

"A couple of things, really," I said. "Do you know anybody by the name of Ransome? Gene Ransome?"

Hurley thought about it. His eyes behind his glasses were a watery blue. "I might've fixed a flat for a fella named Ransome."

"Yesterday?"

"That's right."

"Ever see him before?"

"Don't recall that I ever did."

There was nothing evasive in his tone. He was either a very good liar, or he was telling the truth. I didn't know which. Somebody was lying, either him or Ransome.

"All right," I said. "The other thing is about a truck, one of those jacked-up swamp buggies, a black Ford. You ever see one around here?"

"There's two or three of those around the county. Ain't that right, Temp?"

He looked at his friend, and I thought that I was going to hear him speak, but I was wrong. Temp just looked at Hurley and nodded. Slightly.

"Your brother-in-law's got one of 'em, don't he?" Hurley said.

Another slight nod.

"Fairly common," Hurley said. "I don't see why anybody'd want one, myself. Damn tires cost you a fortune, and if a fella was to be a little drunk he might miss that first step and break his neck. 'Course Temp's brother-in-law don't drink. He's a Babtist."

"Has he been around today?" I said. I looked at Temp. "Your brother-in-law, I mean."

Temp shook his head. Not vigorously.

"Well, that's all I came to ask about. Thanks for your time."

Fred and I started back to the Jeep. Hurley called out to us as we were climbing in.

"I forgot to tell you," he said. "Sheriff's office has one of them big Fords. Use it to get around in the bottoms when the ground's all wet and swampy. Which is a lot of the time around here."

"What do you think?" I asked Fred as we rolled along, the hot breeze blowing in our faces.

"About what?" he said.

"About those trucks."

"Lots of 'em around, like they said."

"Hurley and Temp have access to one. So does Deputy Jackson."

"You really got it in for the deppidy," Fred said.

"I know it," I said. "I guess he rubs me the wrong way, but there are a lot of things about him that bother me."

"He's a lawman," Fred said, as if that settled everything. "He wouldn't mess around with anything illegal, much less a murder."

I thought that was a naïve point of view, but I didn't question it. "What about Temp, then? Who's this brother-in-law of his?"

"Temp's all right, just a little slow. Makes good company for Hurley. His brother-in-law's Dan Bryson. Lives over in the west part of the county. Prob'ly never comes around here if he can help it."

I dropped the subject of the truck, and Fred discussed the property and houses we were passing and made some comments about the owners. When we got fairly near the field where I'd had my encounter, he pointed out a well-kept house that I'd noticed earlier. There was a neatly trimmed yard, and the paint job on the house was fairly recent.

"That's where the Stones live," he said. "Perry and his wife live on down the road a piece."

"How far is this from where Zach Holt lives?" I said.

"Not too far. If you went on past that place where you were this afternoon and turned left instead of right, you'd get down there pretty quick."

I hadn't recognized the turn earlier, but given my state of mind, I supposed I could be excused.

"So the Holt property was close to yours, too," I said.

"That's right. But like I told you, that part's hard to get to. I don't ever go there much, and—" He took his eyes off the road briefly and glanced at me. "What're you gettin' at?"

"I don't know," I said. "What about alligators on that part of your land? Aren't you worried about them as much as you are about the others?"

"Nope. Shouldn't be that many around there. Not that much water. Oh, there's a lot of shallow little pools, places that hold water when it rains, and a few ditches that might've eroded down toward the river, but that's all. Nothin' like what I've got ever'where else."

"I was thinking that Holt might have been poaching back in there, I guess. And I don't have any idea what Ransome would be doing there, or who he might be meeting."

"I don't either," Fred said. "That's why we're gonna check it out. So we can see what's there."

"Isn't there an easier way in? Couldn't we just have gone in from your property, the way we went to look at the dead gator?"

"Could have, I guess. Not a very good way to do it, though. Lots of swampy land in between, hard to cross, even in this Jeep. Mosquitoes you wouldn't believe. In fact, I don't know that we could've made it without gettin' out and walkin'. And then there's the leeches."

'I can see why you don't keep it up too well," I said.

"Yeah. Be interestin' to find out that there's another way in that's easier."

"Even if there is, what would anyone want to do there?"

"Like I said, that's what we're gonna find out."

When he said that, I looked up and saw the tumbled-down house in the field. "Here we are," I said.

He pulled up in front of the house and stopped. We got out and walked over to the remains.

"I remember when the last of the Overtons moved out of this place," Fred said. "Must've been sometime back in the middle fifties. Long time ago."

"Where did they go?" I said.

"Don't know. I drove by here one afternoon and their old broken-down truck was in the yard, kids were runnin' around all over the place, and there was a wash hung out on the line. Few days later, I came back by and there wasn't a cryin' thing here except for the house. They were gone, ever' last one of 'em, and took ever'thing they had with 'em. Never heard of 'em again after that."

"Who owns this land, then?"

"Probably the county's taken it in for taxes by now. Or maybe it's been sold to somebody who doesn't have any interest in it. It's not much, just a few acres—not enough to farm unless you clear the trees, and by the time you got most of the trees cleared, you'd be back to my acreage, which is too swampy to do anything with."

"I guess the Overtons wouldn't recognize the house now," I said.

Looking at the pile of boards sticking crazily this way and that gave me a weak feeling in the knees, especially in the bad one. I could have been in it when it collapsed, and if I had been, I would probably still be there, maybe with a two-by-four sticking halfway through me.

"Looks like one of those Gulf storms hit it," Fred said. "We've had 'em come this far in before. I expect that back in those woods there's trees that were split and bent by the 1900 storm in Galveston."

We both looked up at the late afternoon sky as if expecting to see a hurricane coming in off the Gulf. We didn't, but we did see that the sky was clouding up.

"Looks like we might get us a little shower," Fred said.

There were two things I didn't like about Fred's Jeep. It didn't have a radio, and it didn't have a top.

"Maybe we'd better just forget this," I said.

"You afraid you'll melt if you get wet?"

"I've been wet recently," I said. "I didn't melt, but I got really uncomfortable. And birds shit on me."

"A little water never hurt anybody, and besides that, didn't no birds shit on you," Fred said. "It'll be a while yet before it rains, anyway. Maybe we'll go back in there, see what we came to see, and get out before it starts."

"Exactly what is it that we came to see?"

"Whatever it is that's back in those trees. Whatever it is that your buddy in the Oldsmobile drove back in there to see."

I'd been thinking about that. "Maybe he didn't go back in there to see anything. Maybe he just went to meet somebody."

"I don't think so," Fred said. He stretched out his right arm and pointed. "You see anything funny about those trees where the road goes into 'em?"

It wasn't much of a road, just a set of ruts, and the trees just looked like trees to me. I told Fred that I didn't see anything unusual.

"Yeah, well, I guess that's 'cause you're a city boy. Or maybe I'm just so old and far-sighted I can see better'n you. Look at the limbs."

I looked, but I still didn't see anything.

"Look how they're all broken off or bent back. Somethin' big's been driving back in there. See?"

I saw. I wished I'd brought a pistol. For that matter, I wished I'd brought a cannon.

"What if it's still back there?" I said.

"Only one way to find that out, I guess," Fred said.

I looked at the wreckage of the house. "If there's anyone back there, they aren't going to like it when we come poking our noses in."

"Prob'ly not. But it's likely as not they're on my land, and I don't like the idea of that one bit. I don't like it much more'n I like somebody killin' one of my gators."

"You didn't happen to bring a rifle with you by any chance?" I said.

Fred shrugged. "Didn't think about it."

"I was afraid you'd say that."

"Nobody shot at you today, did they?" he said.

"Not today."

"Nothin' to worry about then. As long as they just try to run over us, we got 'em beat. This Jeep can run away from anything around, even that Ford you're so worried about."

"I'm not worried," I said.

"Sure sounds like it."

"A little nervous, maybe. If you'd been in that house, you'd be a little nervous too."

"Maybe. Well, we goin' or not?"

I looked at the clouds one more time, saw a flash of lightning and heard a low rumble of thunder. I didn't know why I was so leery of going back in the woods. I was the investigator, after all. I shouldn't have to have Fred tell me what we needed to do.

"Why not?" I said.

We got in the Jeep and Fred headed it down the ruts for the woods.

"You can see it don't fit the ruts," Fred said, referring to the Jeep. "They were cut by somethin' a lot bigger."

I could tell, and hearing him say it didn't make me feel any better. I didn't mind trouble so much if I knew what sort of trouble I was getting into, but uncertainty bothered me. I liked to have a plan, even if it wasn't a very good one.

When we got to the trees, the broken branches that Fred had pointed out were much easier to see. The lower limbs, up to about twelve feet, were broken, cracked, and in some places bare of leaves.

"Bobtail truck," Fred said. "Maybe a trailer."

I thought about rustling. "How would rustlers go about getting cows transported?" I said.

"That'd take a trailer, all right," Fred said. "It'd be easy to steal cows, I imagine. Just find a fence you could back up to, cut it, and drive the cows into the trailer. Then you could drive off with 'em and nobody the wiser. At least not till they checked out their stock the next day or the next week. If it was a week, you'd already have sold 'em and stole some more, most likely."

We were into the trees now, and what with the clouds,

almost all the light was cut off. It was almost as if night had suddenly fallen. Fred turned on the headlights, which picked up the ruts in front of us and the trees to the sides.

"You think that's what's going on here?" I said. "Rustling, I mean?"

"Doubt it," he said. "You see any cows around here? Besides, this place's not even fenced."

"I thought maybe someone could be stealing cattle somewhere else and bringing them in here," I said.

"Why would anybody do that?"

"I don't know," I said. "It was just a thought. Perry Stone said something about hearing the trucks at night, and he lives near here."

"Anybody'd be crazy to bring cows back in here. Cows and swamps don't mix too well."

We came to a barbed-wire fence that ran through the trees. It had been cut, and the strands had been pulled back from the ruts, making a wide opening.

"That's my fence," Fred said. "This is for sure my business now."

What he meant was that it was *my* business, but I still couldn't see how it tied in with the dead gator.

"Could anyone get from here to where we found that carcass?" I said.

"Not any easier than I could get from there to here, and that ain't easy. Like I told you."

There was a crash of thunder, and the rain began, not where we were, but farther off. I could hear it rushing through the leaves of the trees, getting closer and closer.

"Sounds like a pretty good one, after all," Fred said.

He was right. When it hit, it sluiced over us in rivulets, even though we were to some extent protected by the trees.

"This road's gonna get real slick, real quick," Fred said. "Good thing we're in the Jeep."

It would have been better not to have been there at all, I thought. I was soaked to the skin in minutes. It was very dark.

Then the trees began to thin out. It was still dark, and the rain was even harder. Through the weeds and water, I could make out a lumpy, uneven terrain, with trees spotted here and there in it, some of them dead and bare of leaves.

The Jeep was sliding a little on the road now. "Here's the swampy part," Fred said.

There were low patches of land, most of them covered with shallow standing water. A real mosquito paradise, I thought. It was hard to see much more than that, even with the headlights.

"Road goes around here," Fred said, turning the Jeep to the right and following the ruts.

We went around a hummock, and the ruts made a wide loop, passing by some more of the standing water and then swinging back into the original track to head back out again.

Fred cut off the engine. "I got a flashlight under the seat," he said, reaching with his right hand. He came up with it, a long black tube that looked as if it would hold three "D" batteries at least. "Waterproof, got a halogen bulb. We'll be able to see a little bit."

He turned it on and waved it from side to side. The beam cut through the rain, all right, but I didn't see anything significant.

Fred turned off the Jeep's headlights, and the darkness sprang to meet us. The flashlight beam was thin but strong as it shone through the rain. I was so wet by now that my short-sleeved sweatshirt was sticking to my chest and back. It felt as if it weighed ten pounds. I knew that when I stepped out of the Jeep my feet would squish wetly in my shoes, even if I were lucky enough to step on solid ground. The way it was raining, solid ground didn't seem like a very good bet.

"Maybe we should have done this in the morning," I said. "We could have seen a good bit better."

"We got to work with what we got," Fred said. "Let's get out and look around."

He swung his legs out of the Jeep.

Well, if an old guy like Fred could take it, so could I. My eyes were getting adjusted to the darkness now, and if we got it over with maybe we wouldn't have to come back.

Fred was standing in front of the Jeep, searching with the light. "You notice anything funny?"

I watched the light carefully, trying to see whatever it was that he could see. I couldn't.

"No," I said.

"Let's walk over this way a little," he said, moving off to the right, keeping the beam in front of him.

I followed along, trying not to step in any holes. Mud oozed around my shoes, and I thought that I would have one hell of a clean-up later. I stepped out of the ruts to the area between them, which was just as wet but not quite as muddy.

"Somebody's been comin' in here for somethin' or other," Fred said. "The ruts don't make any sense otherwise."

I agreed with that, but I couldn't see why anyone would want to be there. There was nothing to see but trees, mostly dead where we were, grass and weeds, and pools of greasy-looking water. Not exactly the kind of spot where anyone would be likely to have a picnic.

"I think the rain's slackin' up a little," Fred said.

He was right. I was so wet that I hadn't noticed, but the main part of the thunderstorm had passed over us. The rain was still pattering down, big drops of it, but not nearly so hard as it had been a few minutes before. Too bad we were already soaked.

"What's that over there?" Fred said, shining the light ahead and to our left.

It was something, all right, sticking up out of a shallow pool of water. I couldn't tell what it was, though, and I didn't particularly want to look at it more closely, since doing so would involve a certain amount of wading.

"What the hell," I said. "I can't get any wetter."

I stepped across the ruts and into the water.

"That's a good place for you to stop," said a voice behind us. "Both of you hold still, or I'll gut-shoot you right here."

I like to think that I'm a semienlightened male, at least in some ways, so it pains me to admit that the thing that bothered me most about the voice was that it belonged to a woman.

$\triangledown$

11

I T'S FUNNY, THE things you think of at a time like that.

I thought of my sister, lying dead in a field for a long, lonely time with no one to know, and of how I'd looked for her for so many months. And how I'd never be absolutely sure of how she got there and why.

I thought of what it would be like to lie there in the rainy darkness with a bullet in my gut.

I thought about how Dino would have to keep on feeding Nameless, and how he'd hate having to do it.

I thought about long blond hair, and a shadow in blue eyes.

"All right," Brenda Stone said. "Put the flashlight down, and then you can both turn around."

Fred bent over and put the light on the ground. We both turned around. Brenda Stone was standing about fifteen yards behind us, holding a small rifle, probably a .22. I didn't think she could kill me with it, not unless she was a really good shot, or unless she got lucky, but it wasn't worth taking the chance. One of those small caliber bullets could tumble around inside me and rearrange my internal organs in a way that the surgeons would never quite figure out.

She looked as if she would shoot without hesitation, too. Her blond hair hung in lank strands around her face, and the man's shirt she was wearing clung to her curves in a way that might have been interesting under other circumstances. Her face was set and hard.

"Can I just step out of this water?" I said.

"Real slow," she said, gesturing slightly with the rifle barrel.

I stepped up to stand beside Fred. "I knew this was a bad idea," I said.

"I knew I shoulda invested in IBM forty years ago," he said.

I got the point.

Brenda looked at us and held the rifle steady. It occurred to me that she didn't have any more of an idea about how to proceed from this point on than I did.

"I guess you know you're trespassing," I said.

"That's not really my problem," she said. "You two are the ones with the problem."

"What exactly *is* the problem?" I said. "That's what I'd like to know."

"You didn't get my husband out of jail," she said.

That wasn't my job, and I hadn't said I'd do it anyhow. But I was a little surprised.

"I talked to him and the sheriff this morning," I said. "I thought he'd be out by now. They didn't really seem to have any grounds for holding him."

"They're holding him," she said.

"What about his alibi?" I said. "What about all those friends of his that he said could vouch for him?"

"Deputy Jackson says friends can lie." She paused thoughtfully. "They probably *are* lying."

"What?" Fred and I said at the same time.

"Perry has a lot of friends. They wouldn't mind lying for him if he killed Zach Holt."

"You mean you think he did it? Why—"

Then it came to me. "You think he might've had a good reason. Those rumors I've heard. They're true."

She didn't say anything, and I accepted her silence as confirmation.

"That still doesn't explain why you're standing there holding a rifle on us," I said. "Can't we go somewhere out of the rain and talk about this?"

"It's not raining," she said.

I was so wet that I hadn't noticed, but she was right. The sky was even beginning to get a little brighter over the tops of the trees, but I knew that it would soon be getting dark again.

"We can walk back over toward your Jeep," she said. "Slow."

Fred and I squished our way toward her as she backed toward the Jeep. She held the rifle on us all the way, the barrel never wavering more than a quarter of an inch. I wondered how she'd gotten down in the woods. I hadn't heard any other vehicles.

"I walked," she said when I asked. "We don't live very far, and I saw you turn in. I thought I recognized Mr. Benton's Jeep."

"That doesn't explain why you're here."

"I'm trying to find out who killed Zach."

"I thought you suspicioned Perry done it," Fred said. "You said his buddies would lie for him."

"I said they'd lie for him. I didn't say he'd done anything. I think he was probably off in the rice fields somewhere yesterday, but I don't think he killed anybody. I think he just got his buddies to say he was with them so he wouldn't get thrown in jail."

"His buddies didn't do him much good, then, did they?" Fred said. "Or maybe they ain't such good buddies after all."

"It's that Jackson," she said. "He's the one. They lied for Perry, all right. He just didn't believe them, and he got one of them to tell the truth. Or I guess that's what happened. Perry didn't know. All he knows is that he's still in jail."

It seemed to me that Jackson was making it look as if Perry Stone were guilty without having all the facts, though it was certainly suspicious that Perry had gotten his friends to lie about his being with them. And of course there was the earlier fight—or scuffle—he'd had with Holt, which added to the reasons for holding him in jail. But why would Stone have killed Holt's wife? Why hadn't Jackson gotten a bullet or two out of the dead alligator? Little things like that bothered me.

"Does your husband know?" I said. "About you and Holt, I mean?"

"No," Brenda said.

She sounded positive, but from my conversation with him that morning, I was sure that Perry had at least heard the rumors.

"What about Holt's wife?" I don't know why I asked. Maybe my mind was constructing some sort of murder-suicide hypothesis.

"She didn't know either. Nobody knew. Until now. Those rumors were just talk for a long time. Zach and I didn't get together until long after they'd already started."

"I hope you weren't planning to shoot us because we know about you and Holt," I said. "We wouldn't have known if you hadn't told us. We didn't come looking to find that out."

"That's what I want to know," she said.

"What?" I said. I couldn't follow her train of thought.

"I want to know what you came looking for."

"We don't know," Fred said.

It was true, but it sounded pretty lame to me, and Brenda Stone didn't take it any differently.

"You mean to tell me you drove down here in the woods in a rainstorm for fun? You must be crazier than a bedbug, then."

"Look," I said. "We're all standing here drenched to the skin, in the dark, in the middle of a swamp." I looked around. "Well, on the edge of a swamp, at least. I'm wet, I'm cold, and I'm uncomfortable. And you're holding a gun on me. Why don't you tell us about why you're here and why you have the rifle. Then we'll tell you why we're here."

She thought about it for a minute. If she'd been some macho guy who felt he had something to prove, she'd have said something like, Hell, no. I've got the gun. You do the talking.

But she was more sensible than that. I liked to think my reasonable argument persuaded her. Maybe it did.

"All right," she said. "I'll tell you. First of all, you have to understand about Zach. He wasn't happy with his wife. She didn't like the way they lived, and she was always complaining."

It was such an old story that it might even have been true. Whether it was or not didn't matter. It had been true enough for Brenda Stone.

"We happened to meet on the road one day," she said. "Just passed in our cars. So we stopped and talked for a little while. We'd gone together before, a long time ago, and one thing just led to another."

Another old story. So was what came next.

"It wasn't that I loved him or anything. It was just that—I don't know. Being married to Perry was fine. He's really very nice. But we never *go* anywhere. We never *do* anything. We live out here in the middle of nowhere, and his idea of a good time is to go down to the river and set out a trotline for yellow cat. You'd think we could go into Houston now and then, go to a movie, go out to eat at a nice place. But we never do. We watch TV, we make popcorn, we—"

She stopped herself and shook her head. "I didn't mean to go into all that. But you can see why what happened . . . happened. Sometimes Zach and I would meet in that old house up there. What happened to that house?"

I thought about that mattress. I hadn't been the only one who used it, and now I knew why it had been there.

"I'll tell you about the house when it's my turn," I said. "I still don't know what you're doing here."

"I think you killed Zach," she said. "And if you did, I'm going to kill you."

I wasn't convinced that she could do it.

If we both rushed her, one of us could get to her even if

the other was shot; and if he was shot only once or twice, whoever took the bullets stood a fair chance of surviving.

Not that I wasn't worried. And not that I wanted to be the one who took the bullets. I didn't want Fred to get shot, either, but that was beside the point. The whole thing would be easier if we could convince Brenda Stone that killing us was simply a bad idea.

"It's pretty dark," I said. "Do you think you could hit us?"

"Perry's taught me to shoot. I can hit you."

"Fine," I said.

"Fine, hell," Fred said. "I say we take that peashooter away from her and beat her over the head with it."

"Don't try it," she said.

It was almost too dark now to make out the rifle barrel, but I would have bet that it was pointed in Fred's general direction. I decided to try again.

"We didn't kill Zach," I said.

"I didn't expect you to admit it," she said.

"Why do you think we did?" I said. "What have we done besides drive down here to the woods? We're not even on your land. You're the trespasser, and now you're talking about murder. You're going to wind up in jail along with Perry."

"I could dump you in one of these holes back here, drive that Jeep in after you, and nobody'd find you till the year 2000," she said.

For someone with worried blue eyes, she was certainly cold-blooded. "You're probably right," I said, thinking that she had a point. If there was quicksand, or if the water were deep enough to cover the Jeep, she was certainly right. I was glad I hadn't waded any farther into the water before she stopped me.

"You still haven't answered my question," I said.

"Which one was that?"

"Why do you think we're the ones who killed Zach Holt?"

"Because he knew something."

Fred snorted. "I say she's crazy. I say we jump her."

"If we decide to do that, let's don't warn her first," I said.
To Brenda I said, "What did he know?"

"He didn't tell me."

Fred muttered something I didn't catch.

"So we killed him for something he knew, but you don't
have any idea what that was. Is that right?"

"Yes."

"Then why do you think we know what it is?"

"Because you're down here."

Fred muttered again. This time I caught the words "crazy
as hell."

I didn't think so. Confused maybe, but not crazy. I wished
I could see her better, watch her face. That would make
things easier, I thought.

"Being down here has something to do with Zach's death,
right?"

"Now you're getting it," she said. "He told me that there
was something here that was going to make us rich. We were
going to leave here and go to someplace better. Someplace
where he didn't have to spend all his time doing dirty work
like skinning alligators and where we could go out to eat and
see a movie every now and then."

"You know about anything here that could do that for a
man, Fred?" I said.

"Nope," he said. "Nothing out here but mosquitoes and
snakes."

I wished he hadn't said that about the snakes. It was one
thing to have the bugs on your neck, which I did, singing in
my ear and then biting me—or was it the ones that didn't
sing that bit you?—but it was something else again to worry
about snakes.

"There was something here," Brenda said. "Zach said he
knew about it."

While her attention was on Fred, I took a step to the side.
She didn't notice; it was too dark, and I moved slowly.

"There *is* something about this place," I said.

And there was. I didn't know what it was but there was

something that wasn't right, something that didn't fit with the surroundings.

"I'm gettin' real cold," Fred said, getting Brenda's attention again.

I'd already noticed that he had better night vision than I did, and I was sure he'd seen me edging away from him. It didn't seem quite fair that he could see better than I could, considering the difference in our ages, but I wasn't going to worry about it. I slid farther away from him.

"We didn't kill Zach," he said. "And we don't even know what you're talkin' about. So why don't we forget this ever happened and go somewhere that we can get warm? I'm goin' to catch pneumonia and die, even if you don't shoot us."

"I don't believe you," she said.

"Look here," Fred said. "Somebody tried to kill us the other day. Took a few shots at us from the woods on my place. We want to know about Zach as much as you do, 'cause somebody's after us too. And we want to get Perry out of jail. What you need to think about now is Perry, not about gettin' revenge on who killed Zach. All that's gonna get you is a cell in the state pen."

"What about the money Zach told me about?"

I have to admit that my opinion of Brenda Stone had lowered a great deal in the last fifteen minutes or so. She was a very pretty woman, but she was also unfaithful to her husband and greedy to boot. It was a real shame, but that's the way it works out sometimes. I'd felt sorry for her and wanted to help her that morning. Now I just wanted to jerk the rifle out of her hands and send her home.

Well, I wasn't going to get a better opportunity. She was listening to Fred, I had managed to separate myself from him by a pretty good distance, and he was ready for me to try something.

So I did. I planted my good leg and charged Brenda.

She saw me coming, but not until it was too late. I hit her high, getting my hands on the rifle and twisting the barrel up. The gun went off, a typical .22 pop, and I smelled the burned powder as we fell to the ground, me on top.

Her breath went out in a whoosh, and I jerked the rifle away from her and tossed it in the general direction of Fred, hoping he'd have the presence of mind to pick it up.

Brenda gasped for breath and twisted under me, struggling to swing her arms. I tried to pin them to her sides, and we slopped in the mud.

Under other circumstances it might have been fun. If I hadn't heard what she'd been saying recently. If she hadn't threatened to kill me. Now I didn't like her very much.

We struggled briefly, and then she went limp. There wasn't much fight in her.

Or so I thought. When I started to lift myself off her, she came up with a sharp knee toward my groin, and I barely managed to twist aside in time, taking the kneecap on the outside of my thigh. I'd have a bruise tomorrow.

"That'll be enough of that," Fred said. "I got the rifle now."

I rolled on over and got up, dripping water and mud, looking a little bit like the Creature from the Black Lagoon.

Brenda just lay on the muddy ground. She was crying. Earlier, that might have bothered me. Now it didn't seem to matter so much. Still, I bent over to help her up.

She slugged me in the jaw as hard as she could, twisting away and slithering off through the mud, trying to get to the other side of the Jeep. I knew that Fred was too much of a gentleman of the old school to actually shoot her, so I dived at her, getting my arms wrapped around her legs and bringing her down into the mud again. I hit her in the back of the head, and her face slapped into the mud and she was still.

Not that I trusted her.

"If she tries anything else, Fred, shoot her," I said as I stood up. "Or give me the gun, and I'll shoot her."

He handed me the .22. "Rifle," he said.

"Rifle. I'll try to remember. Do you have any rope stashed in that Jeep?"

"I'll see," he said. "Let me find the flashlight."

He splashed off to where we'd been standing earlier, and in a minute or so the beam of the flashlight came on, focusing on Brenda Stone.

She was sitting up now, and she blinked in the light. Otherwise, she didn't move.

"See about that rope," I told Fred.

While he rummaged around under the seats in the Jeep, I talked to Brenda.

"We're going to have to tie you up," I said. "I hate to have to do it, but you don't seem very trustworthy." I rubbed my jaw where she'd slugged me. She had quite a punch. "After we get all cleaned up and dried off, we're going to have a little chat about things."

She was a dark shape on the ground. I couldn't see the expression on her face, if there was one.

"We're not going to turn you in to the sheriff," I said. "I don't really have any hard feelings about this, and I don't think Fred does either. But you've got to understand that we didn't kill your boyfriend and that we don't know who did. And you don't have to worry about your husband. We're not going to confirm the rumors for him. That's your business unless it turns out that Perry actually did kill Holt. The it's our problem, or it is if it ties in to whatever's going on here on this property, which I guess it does."

"Here's the rope," Fred said, coming over with the light.

He was holding a thin strand of nylon rope that had once been white. It was hard to say exactly what color it was now. In the dark, it looked black and oily, as if it had been under the seat in the Jeep for a long time.

"Tie her up," I said. "Just her hands ought to be enough."

Fred handed me the light, and I held it in my left hand with the rifle in my right. I turned the beam of the flashlight on Brenda, who looked as if she wanted to cry some more. Or maybe she just wanted to spit on us. It was hard to tell. She did neither, however, as Fred tied her hands behind her back.

"All right," I said. "Let's all get in the Jeep."

Fred and I got Brenda into the passenger seat, and then
Fred got behind the wheel. I sat behind Brenda on a tool box
and held the rifle.

"Now where to?" Fred said.

"If Perry's still in jail, we might as well go to his house,"
I said. "No one's likely to bother us there, and you can call
Mary to tell her we haven't been eaten by a giant gator."

Fred started the Jeep and slewed it around in the mud,
heading it back out toward the road.

"We still don't know what's goin' on here," he said.

"I'm beginning to get an idea, though," I told him. "Let's
go get dry."

$\triangledown$

12

W HEN WE GOT to Brenda's house, Fred called Mary while I showered and changed into some of Perry's clothes. They were too tight and too short, but they would have to do. Then I watched Brenda while Fred cleaned up. Brenda would get her turn later, if I thought we could trust her.

"We're not going to tell anyone about this, Brenda," I said. "We don't want you and Perry to get into any more trouble than you already have."

I didn't know whether she would buy me as an understanding, sympathetic character. After all, I was the one who'd wrestled her to the ground and hit her in the back of the head after she'd tried to knee me and deck me with her fist. But I was telling the truth. It wasn't the time to cause any more trouble.

She was wet and muddy, with dark streaks of mud in her blond hair, made darker now by the dampness and by it sticking together in thick strands.

"I don't know why I did it," she said. "I just thought that somehow I ought to do something for Zach."

And find out about the money, I thought. Brenda was still looking for a way out, and if Zach couldn't go with her, well, she would probably be willing to go alone.

It wasn't that I blamed her much. I'd seen myself for the last year, and my friend Dino for a lot more years than that, burying ourselves in a place that almost allowed us to forget that the outside world existed.

The trouble was that the outside world had a way of intruding, and then you had to do something about it. Brenda wasn't like us. She was young and eager; she didn't want to be buried so long before her time.

Fred came into the room, toweling his hair. Fred's body was thinner than mine, and Perry Stone's clothing hung loosely on him. He didn't have much hair, either, and it didn't take him long to get it dry.

"All right," he said, tossing the towel on a chair. "What do we do now?"

We were sitting at the kitchen table, which was round, with a yellow Formica top. Fred pulled up a chair, not the one he'd tossed the towel on, and joined us. The chairs had yellow vinyl seats and backs and were made of some kind of tubular steel. It wasn't the most expensive dinette set I'd ever seen.

"We have to decide what to do with Mrs. Stone," I said. "Then we go home and get a good night's sleep."

"Shoulda shot her while we were back in the woods," Fred said. "That's what she was gonna do to us."

Fred sometimes had a dry way of putting things, and it was hard to tell whether he meant them or not. Considering what he had said when Brenda was holding the rifle on us, I thought he might be serious.

So did Brenda. "I wasn't going to shoot you. I really wasn't. I just wanted to scare you. To find out what happened to Zach."

Maybe she really believed that, but I didn't.

Fred didn't either. He said, "Somebody shot Zach, that's what happened. And I'd like to know who did it just as much as you would. From what you were sayin' not so long ago, I think old Perry might be involved more than I thought he was."

It was hard for me to see that Perry could have been involved. I'd talked to him, and he just didn't seem the kind of man to get mixed up in murder. He was a little hotheaded, but he had fought Zach with his fists, not with a gun.

On the other hand, Brenda was a good-looking woman, and Perry *had* gotten his friends to lie for him. Or he had if Brenda was to be believed.

That's the way it always is in life. You never knew who was telling the truth. Sometimes the people who were talking to you didn't even know they were lying. They were telling what they thought was the truth, and they believed it.

"I think we should forget the whole thing," I said.

They both looked at me.

"I mean it," I said. "We just go home and forget it."

"Why?" Fred said. "For all we know, she's the one who shot at us the other day. She might take a notion to do it again if we let her get away with this."

"That bullet I dug out of the dead gator didn't come from any .22, did it?"

"Well, no, but—"

"So that was somebody else. And Brenda wouldn't come after us again. Would you, Brenda?"

She shook her head, swinging the dirty blond hair. "No," she said. "No, I wouldn't do that."

I looked at Fred. "See? She wouldn't do it again."

"You believe her?"

"Sure," I said, though I wasn't really sure. "She'd never be able to get both of us, and we'll tell Mary when we get back to your place. That'll make three of us who know. And if one of us has an accident or gets shot, the others can tell the sheriff. And they can tell Perry about his wife and Zach."

"I won't do anything," Brenda said. "I promise."

This time, I believed her.

The next morning I was in the county library, looking through back issues of both Houston newspapers. There was something I'd read a few weeks back that had nudged at the corners of my memory while we were standing there in the rain with Brenda, and I wanted to see if I could find the article again.

It took over an hour of digging, but I didn't mind. It was much more pleasant than the other ways I'd been spending my time lately—getting shot at while lying in a swampy lake, getting chased by a Paleolithic truck, standing in the rain while being threatened by a woman with a rifle.

I finally located the article I was looking for, though I almost missed it. It was on one of the inside pages, and though it was three columns wide, it was still fairly brief. It was about PCBs being found in disposal pits beside natural gas pipelines.

I asked the librarian if I could make a copy, and she showed me how to use the machine. I finally got the paper in the right position, put in my coin, and pressed the right button. The copy was a bit dark, but it was still easily readable.

Fred was not impressed when I showed it to him.

"I don't see what this has to do with a damned thing," he said.

"I'm not sure that it fits in," I said. "But last night I noticed that something was funny about the place we were in. I couldn't figure out what, at first, but then it came to me. It was the smell."

Fred thought about that. "I guess I noticed that, too, a little bit. But it smells like that around here ever' now and then, when the wind's right."

"There wasn't much wind last night, and it was raining. We're going to have to go back and check anyway. Maybe this time we won't be interrupted."

"So what you're sayin' is that somebody's dumping chemicals on my land."

"Yes. I think that was a barrel of some kind that I was wading out to look at before Brenda Stone got the drop on us."

"Could've been, I guess. You might not be so quick to wade out there again, I bet."

I hadn't been so quick the first time, the way I remembered it. Maybe this time I'd wear hip boots.

Fred looked at the copy of the article again. "This here says they weren't dumpin' the stuff on anybody's land. Says they were buryin' it right there beside the pipelines."

"They got caught at that," I said. "Maybe they found a new place to get rid of it. Or maybe it's someone else."

"Oh. What is this stuff, anyway, this PCB?"

"Polychlorinated biphenyls," I said. "It might cause cancer."

"And they put that stuff on my property?"

"We don't know for sure, but one of those pipelines isn't too far from here. And one of those companies is Wessey Gas. You've seen their signs, haven't you?"

"They're all over. Can't miss 'em."

"All of them are red, green, and blue, too. The same colors that barrel looked to be."

"Pretty farfetched," Fred said.

Maybe it was, but it all fit.

"Why'd anybody use those poly-whatevers in the first place?" he said.

"It's used as some kind of flame retardant," I said.

He thought some more. "I guess it's worth checkin' out, then."

"It's better than anything else we've got."

"I still don't see what that's got to do with killin' my gator," he said.

"Me neither," I said.

As it turned out, I did the checking on my own. After all, I was the hired hand. Besides, I thought it would be a good idea to leave someone behind to call in the troops in case I disappeared. I was going to be very careful, but you never knew what might happen. But most of all I wanted to do a little more talking before I did the checking, the kind of talking that I could do best if Fred stayed behind.

He argued about it, but eventually he gave in. He could see the logic of my reasoning.

"But you better be back here by seven o'clock," he said. "Eight at the latest, or I'm callin' the sheriff."

That was all right with me. "You know where to send him," I said.

Fred let me take the Jeep, since it would still be pretty messy in the woods and beyond. The Subaru, with its front-wheel drive, would probably have made it through, but it would have gotten so muddy I might not have recognized it. The Jeep, on the other hand, was already in that condition, with thick clumps of mud in the wheel wells and on the bumpers and sides.

"It stays that way most of the time," Fred told me. "I cleaned it up before you came, but it'll run just fine while it's muddy. It always does. I'll clean it up again next year."

So I felt like a real off-road backwoodsman as I pulled up in front of Hurley Eckles's store and station. It was one of those rare nice days when the humidity was lower than the temperature. The rain showers had been caused by the leading edge of a cold front, which had blown through during the night, carrying the moisture in the air along with it.

A less pleasant side effect was the high wind, which swooshed through the trees and made them sound a little like waves on the Gulf. It was so windy that no one was sitting outside at Hurley's place.

I got out of the Jeep and went inside. The store wasn't very well stocked, just a couple of wooden shelves with the necessities of life: toilet paper, Vienna sausage, Ranch Style Beans. Things like that. There were two stacks of new tires and a cooler for beer and soft drinks. No milk or anything that might spoil. The ceiling was low, and there were a couple of fluorescent tubes for light. There was a short counter with an old cash register on it.

Hurley and his buddy Temp were sitting in two lawn chairs in front of the counter. The chairs were made of aluminum tubing and plastic webbing that was old and ragged. The bottom of Hurley's chair sagged, and a strand of the webbing hung down to the floor.

"You gettin' to be a regular customer of mine," Hurley said. " 'Cept you don't ever buy nothin'."

Temp grinned at his pal's wit. One of these days he was going to break down and say something. It was an event I was looking forward to.

"Just dropped in for some more friendly conversation," I said.

"You bring that Fred Benton along for company?"

"Not this time."

Hurley spit on the floor, which was made of concrete and stained a snuffy brown all round the chair. Well, it was his store.

"What you want to talk about this time?" he said.

"Rustlers," I said. "Illegal killing of alligators. Things like that."

"That horse turd," Hurley said.

"Which one is that?" I said.

"That damn Fred Benton, that's which one. He don't never let a man forget, and he don't never forgive."

"How's that?" I said.

"One time," Hurley said. "*One*. That's all it takes to get a man like Fred Benton on your case for life. That horse turd."

"One time for what?"

Hurley spit and sighed. Temp sighed too, whether in sympathy or just as an echo, I couldn't tell. I was just glad to know he could make a sound.

"Look," Hurley said. "This is the way it is. Me and Fred don't get along, and it all comes down to one thing." He stared at me, his watery eyes sincere behind his glasses. "Gators."

"Gators?"

"That's what I said. Gators. He likes 'em. I don't. That's what it all comes down to."

"You're trying to tell me that you and Fred have a philosophical disagreement?"

"I don't know what the hell that means," he said, pushing

his hat up on his head. People like Hurley would no more think about taking their hats off indoors than I would of exposing myself onstage at Carnegie Hall. "Let me put it this way. There ain't a man in this whole area that ain't killed him a gator once or twice. There was a time when it was purely illegal, no season or nothin', but if you could kill one and sell the skin, you could get good money for it. And there's been a time or two when most people around here could use a little money."

He leaned forward in the chair. "Not Fred, though. 'Course not. He's always had plenty. But the rest of us? Sure. So why not get it the best way you know how? If that means killin' a gator, well, that's just the way it is. A gator ain't nothin' but a big lizard that's lived way beyond its time, anyway. Those things ought to've died off way back in the prehistoric days."

He looked over at Temp as if seeking support for his argument. Temp looked back but kept quiet.

"What're they good for, huh?" Hurley said. "They do anything good for anybody? 'Course not. They kill animals, probably even calves, but they don't *do* anything worth a damn. So what's wrong with killin' one?"

"They're an endangered species," I said, the words sounding as if I'd learned them on a PBS documentary, which I probably had.

"Who gives a shit?" He spit again. "If they was all gone, who'd miss 'em, 'cept for Fred Benton?"

I didn't answer him. I thought I'd miss them, but what did I know? Maybe I wouldn't even care. I hear on the news that we're losing any number of species every day as the South American rain forests are being destroyed for timber, and it bothers me, but I haven't actually done much mourning.

"Anyhow, that's what it's all about," Hurley said. "Fred's been after me ever since, and he's accused me of ever'thing that's happened, too. I think he blames me for the Vietnam War, ever' hurricane that hits the coast, and AIDS."

"I don't think he'd go quite that far," I said. "And you still haven't told me exactly what you're talking about."

"All right, I'll tell you. One time, *one*, I killed a gator. It happened to be on Fred's land, and I didn't want him to know it, but he found out about it. I needed the money bad, so I did it. And that was it. Never before, never since. But he still holds it against me."

"When was this?" I said.

"Hell, I don't know." He looked at Temp. "Twenty years ago?"

Temp nodded.

"At least twenty years ago. Maybe more."

Temp nodded again.

Well, I wasn't surprised, exactly. Fred was a man who had a way of holding grudges, and he did like alligators.

"So that's why he's got it in for me," Hurley said. "After all this time, he won't let it go. But I'll tell you this. I didn't kill any gator on his place in the last twenty years, I didn't kill Zach Holt or his wife, and I ain't no rustler. So how's that?"

I told him that was fine with me. "But you've heard about rustling around here?"

"Sure. Ever'body's heard about it. Don't mean I did it."

"I didn't mean to say you had. What I'd like to know is, who's losing all the cattle?"

Hurley thought about it. Even Temp looked as if he might be thinking. Or trying to.

"Come to think of it, I don't know," Hurley said. "That's kind of funny, ain't it?"

"Funny?"

"Funny strange, not funny ha-ha," he said. "You'd think I'd know a thing like that."

"You sure would," I said. "If anybody's been losing cattle, that is."

"Far as I know, not a single soul's said a word about that part of it. I wonder why that is?"

"What *have* they said?"

He thought it over.

Temp thought it over, too, or seemed to. With him it was hard to tell one way or the other.

"I guess what they've talked about is the trucks," Hurley said.

"What trucks?"

"The cattle trucks. They come by on the county roads at night. Ever'body hears 'em."

"If you hear them but don't see them, how do you know that they're cattle trucks? Especially if there aren't any cattle missing?"

"I don't know," Hurley said. "What other kind of trucks would there be back in here?"

I had an idea about that, but I still wondered why everyone seemed to think there was rustling going on.

Then Hurley came up with the answer. "I think it was that Deppidy Jackson. I remember he was in here one day drinkin' a Coke. I remember he was the one that asked if there was rustlin' goin' on around here."

Somehow, I wasn't surprised.

▽

13

I DIDN'T DRIVE down the ruts that wound into the woods.

First, I drove by the collapsed house to see if anything was stirring. Nothing was. Then I drove the Jeep into the same clump of bushes where I'd parked the Subaru the day before, but because I'd already made an opening I had to break off a few branches to cover the Jeep, or at least try to conceal it from a casual glance.

It always looks easy when someone does that in the movies, but they must be dealing with a much more brittle type of tree. It was quite a struggle to get even one or two limbs of any size broken off, so I just did my best and hoped it would get by. I didn't really think anyone would be looking for me.

I also made sure not to walk down the rutted road. Instead, I angled in through the woods, hoping that I had enough woodsy skills to enable me to find the right spot.

It was a doubtful proposition, since most of my woodcraft had been gleaned from various old issues of *Walt Disney's Comics and Stories*, particularly the ones in which Huey, Dewey, and Louie participated in the Junior Woodchucks. Still, it seemed like a relatively simple task, at least compared to something like finding the North Star and using it to guide you halfway across the continent, which escaped slaves had once done.

The rain the previous evening had made the ground mushy, and the walking wasn't especially pleasant, particularly with the wind whipping around in the treetops above me. There were no animal or bird sounds to distract me, or if there were I didn't hear them above the sound of the wind.

I slogged along, trying to keep my footing and trying hard to avoid slapping myself in the face with low-hanging limbs. After a few minutes, I was almost as wet as I had been the night before. In the shade under the trees, the water hadn't evaporated or been blown off the leaves by the wind, and a lot of it wound up on my clothes.

I know that the health gurus say that you can't catch a cold merely by getting your clothes wet or by sitting in a draft or by getting a chill, and I suppose they must be right. I'd gotten wet more often in the last few days than ever before in my life, outside of a bathtub or the Gulf, anyway, and I was still healthy. On the other hand, I had a strong feeling that I was pushing my luck.

While I was trying to walk in a straight line, my thoughts tended to wander a bit. I found myself thinking of Jan again and wondering what her last moments must have been like. It was pure morbidity on my part, but no matter how many times I told myself that I wasn't to blame for her death, I was never completely convinced. Especially considering the dying words of a former friend of mine. I suppose it's barely possible that you can be to blame for things you know nothing about, and if that's true, then I was to blame.

I was as much to blame as Oedipus was, to take a literary example, or that was one way to look at it. Not the most cheerful way, admittedly, but *a* way.

The good thing about worrying about Fred's dead alligator and everything else that had been happening to me was that I didn't have much spare time to contemplate fate and free will or to feel guilty about something I could do nothing about. I had been doing too much of that for too long a time.

Maybe after this job I would look for something else to do. Painting houses was all right, and the work wasn't difficult, but it gave me too much time to think. Standing in rain-dark swamps with wet blonds holding rifles on me had the beneficial effect of taking my mind off my other troubles.

I brought myself back to the task at hand. The problem with a rambling mind is that your feet tend to ramble as well, and if that happens, you lose your way.

I had lost mine, as I realized after I'd been walking for far longer than it should have taken me to find the pool with the barrel in it.

I decided to retrace my steps, and then I realized that I should have marked the trail in some way if I ever wanted to find it again. Even a pair of kids as young as Hansel and Gretel had known that. I hoped the Junior Woodchucks didn't hear about this.

Of course I hadn't thought I'd get lost.

It had seemed like a simple thing to spot the road, angle toward it, and meet it at about the place where I'd seen the barrel. That way, nobody would see me coming if there was anyone there, and I would be able to sneak up and spy out the ground before revealing myself.

It was a fine idea.

It would have been even finer if it had worked. The half-forgotten words of Robert Burns flitted through my mind, the ones about mice and men and what often happens to their plans.

I looked around me. There were a lot of trees, all of which looked more or less alike to me. There aren't any trees on Galveston Island.

Well, that's an exaggeration. There are palm trees, and even a few others. But damned few. Not enough, anyway, to inspire a young man growing up there to become an amateur botanist in his spare time.

I thought I recognized a pecan tree and an oak, or lots of pecans and lots of oaks. But maybe I was wrong. It didn't make much of a difference, anyway, since I hadn't taken notice of any of the trees I'd been passing in the first place.

If I were Kit Carson or one of those old scouts, I could have looked for footprints, but . . .

I realized that I could still do that. Thank goodness for muddy ground. It didn't take me long to find places where I'd walked, my feet sinking into the soft ground, and other places where I'd skidded slightly and shoved a fair-sized chunk of earth aside.

I followed my path backward and saw that I'd been making a circle, the classic example of what happens to an unskilled person wandering around in the woods. To be sure it didn't happen again, I went almost all the way back to the Jeep, stopping when I was within sight of it.

Then I followed the ruts. To hell with woodcraft. I wasn't going to get lost again, and if it meant taking a chance on being seen, that was just the way it would have to be. The best I could do was to stay to the side of the ruts, partially concealed in the trees, but never getting so far from the track that I couldn't see it. Even if the wind didn't die down, I would be able to hear a truck coming and have enough time to hide myself before it got to where I was.

As I walked along, I realized that getting lost had served the same purpose as working for Fred: it had taken my mind off other things. It's amazing what a little bit of distraction can do for a person.

After fifteen minutes or so I got to the place where the trees began to thin out. I had to walk in the road when I got to the fence, not feeling like slithering under it or trying to climb between the wires. I knew that if I did either of those things, I'd probably snag my jeans or shirt. Seeing the fence made me feel better, though. I knew that I was going in the right direction. When I'd made the circle, I'd managed to miss the fence entirely, having begun my turning before I ever got to it.

Things in the clearing looked different in the daylight. I could see a kind of green scum on top of the pool of water I'd waded into, and the water itself seemed almost opaque.

The chemical smell lingered in the air, even with a wind that would have seemed capable of driving it away.

The barrel, on the other hand, was gone.

There were any number of good reasons why the barrel might not be there, I thought.

It could have sunk down beneath the green, greasy water.

It could have dissolved because of the chemical it contained.

A giant mutant frog could have swallowed it.

Or someone could have come and moved it.

For one reason or another, I favored the latter possibility. The question that remained was, who had moved it? And when? And why? Aside from those things, the only other thing I wanted to know was whether there were any more barrels around.

I started looking. There were a number of places near the water that looked as if they'd been recently disturbed, and it was possible that barrels could be buried there. There was no way I could find out, however. I hadn't brought a shovel, and I wasn't going to dig with my hands.

I didn't blame myself for lack of foresight. How was I to know that the barrel would be gone? To me, it had seemed a simple matter of going back and retrieving it.

I walked around the marshy area, looking for an open hole, a place where the barrels hadn't been covered yet, if there were any more of them there at all. I didn't see anything like what I was looking for.

It was time to go wading again, I supposed. There was nothing else left, except to dig with my hands, and I still didn't want to do that. I'd just have to splash out into the water and see if the barrel had sunk, or if there were any others.

I thought about snakes and quicksand, wished that I hadn't, and waded into the pool.

I found a barrel almost immediately, by the simple method of bumping into it. I jumped about a foot out of the water, thinking I'd hit an alligator, but I recovered quickly and pulled the barrel to the surface. It was unmarked. So was the second one I found.

Two were enough. I suspected that if I found others, they would also be unmarked. I'd been lucky enough to spot the one marked with the Wessey Gas colors the night before, though there might be others buried nearby, and now it was gone.

I slopped out of the pool, wondering what kind of terrible destructive and corrosive chemicals had leaked into the marsh and then been transported onto my body by the water. I hadn't noticed any tadpoles or minnows swimming around. I told myself that the water was too dark, and I just hadn't been able to see them beneath the surface.

I stood on a relatively dry patch of ground, letting the water drain down my pants legs and out of my shoes. Where in hell had that marked barrel gone?

It wasn't in the pool, or I would have found it.

Fred hadn't taken it, and I hadn't. I could vouch for us.

That left Brenda Stone. She had been there when I was after it, and she had probably seen what I was going for. I couldn't vouch for her.

On the other hand, I didn't think she'd taken the barrel. I'd talked pretty straight to her, and I'd believed her when she said she'd keep quiet about what happened. I didn't think she would have returned for the barrel.

She wouldn't be the first person who'd ever told me a lie and made me believe it, however, or who had fooled me by doing something I hadn't expected. I'd have to talk to her again.

Keeping off to the side of the ruts, I sloshed back to the Jeep.

Brenda Stone looked a lot better when she was clean and dry, and the shadows were black in her blue eyes again. Even knowing what I did about her, I had a few thoughts that I'm sure her husband wouldn't have appreciated.

"I didn't say anything to anybody," she told me. "Really. I promised, and I didn't say a word."

I had managed to get most of the mud off my shoes, and my clothes were practically dry. I was sitting on a small sofa with deep cushions, and I kept sinking farther and farther into them.

"Think about it," I said. "You've been to see Perry today, I'm sure."

"Yes," she said. "I've been to see him."

She looked away from me, but I didn't know whether she did so to hide a lie or because she was embarrassed at what I knew about her and Zach Holt, a secret that I was virtually certain she hadn't shared with Perry, no matter what his suspicions might have been.

"You must have talked about something," I said.

"Well, we talked about how he didn't like jail and how it wasn't right for him to be there."

"What's his bond set for? Maybe we can get him bailed out."

"It's fifty thousand dollars. Perry says that's too much and that we oughtn't to put it up. The lawyer's trying to get it reduced, but Perry says jail's not as bad as getting gouged for money by a bondsman."

He might change his mind after a few more days, but whatever he decided was fine with me. It was his life.

"Has the lawyer found out what kind of evidence they've got to justify holding him?" I said.

The shadows in her eyes deepened. "It's a gun."

"A gun?" I said. Nobody at the jail had mentioned a gun to me.

"They say they found it behind the seat in his pickup. It's a pistol, but Perry says it's not his."

"When did this happen?"

"Yesterday afternoon, I guess. Before they were going to let him out."

That seemed very convenient to me. "Who found the pistol?"

"I don't know," she said. "I think the lawyer said it was that deputy. Jackson."

What a surprise, I thought. "And Perry says the pistol's not his?"

"He says not. I know I've never seen him with one, and he never told me he had one." She looked at me directly this time. "You can help him, can't you?"

A few looks from her like that one, and I'd be offering to take Zach Holt's place and carry her away from all this.

"I don't know," I said. "Maybe the gun isn't the one that was used in the murders. They'll have to get ballistics tests run on it before they know."

"That's what they're doing now, the lawyer says. He says they've sent the gun to Houston. Perry says it's not his gun in the first place, and he doesn't care what the tests say." She shook her head. "I don't see how all of this got so complicated."

I didn't either. The pistol would make good evidence if it turned out to be the murder weapon, and I had a strong feeling that it would. Perry Stone was getting wrapped up very tightly in a web that he wasn't going to be able to escape from easily.

"What about fingerprints?" I said. "Were there any prints on the gun?"

"I don't know. Perry didn't say."

"Maybe not then. That's a good sign."

"Why?"

"Perry can say they planted the gun in his truck. A jury might not believe him, but if his prints aren't on the gun, no one can prove who put it there." I had my own thoughts on that subject, but I didn't voice them.

"Oh," she said, ducking her head.

Her hair fell forward over her shoulders. She was a very attractive woman, and I found myself hoping that she and Perry could work things out. It was really none of my business, but I hoped it anyway.

"With Perry telling you all this, I guess you didn't have time to talk to him much about last night," I said.

"No, not really." She looked away.

"But you probably told him a little."

"Just a little." Her gaze went past me and out the window at my back, out into the fields across the road.

"How much?"

"I told him that I heard some cars down there and saw some lights." She looked back at me. "I told him that I got scared and wished he was at home. That's all."

"You're sure?"

She stood up. Her body was stiff, and the blue eyes sparked. A flush rose up her neck and spread over her face. Her voice rose almost to a shout.

"What did you want me to say? That I went down there looking for the men who killed Zach? That I wanted to kill them because they'd murdered the man I slept with?"

Her anger surprised me, coming as it did so suddenly and without warning. She had been sitting quietly, almost submissively, until the anger had broken through.

"That's not what I meant," I said. "I meant, did you tell him about seeing anything down there. You could have investigated the lights and seen something."

"I didn't, though. I told him that I locked all the doors and thought about how I needed him here at home."

She sat back down, her anger gone as quickly as it had come. Her voice sank, and the flush faded from her cheeks. I almost doubted that I'd seen it, though I knew I had.

"And you didn't say anything to anyone else?"

"No. I haven't even *seen* anyone else. What difference does it make, anyway?"

"None," I said. "I was just wondering."

I was still wondering when I left. The only thing to do now was to talk about it to Perry, and I had to do that without revealing what had happened between me and his wife. I had threatened to tell him that the rumors about Zach Holt were true, but I would never really do that.

At least I didn't think I would. There might come a time when my scruples would relax enough to allow it, but I didn't think it would be any time soon.

It wasn't that I thought so much of Brenda Stone. She was beautiful, almost, but that didn't really have any influence on me. It was just that I felt sorry for her husband, and maybe what had happened would change both him and her enough for them to have a chance together if I could help get Perry out of jail. It wouldn't be much of a chance, given Brenda's past actions, but it was a chance of some kind.

I wondered about Brenda. Her sudden anger, the way she had flared up with no warning, bothered me. It was the kind of thing that could result in thoughtless and even dangerous action, given the right circumstances.

What if she had visited Zach Holt, and his wife had discovered them?

What if she had gone to Holt's house to confront him and demand that he take her away from all this swampland and that he do it immediately? And what if he had refused?

If there had been a gun handy, she might very well have used it. Her anger at me had been that strong. And if Holt's wife had walked in, well, too bad for her, too.

But why would Brenda Stone have killed and skinned an alligator on Fred Benton's place? There was no reason that I could think of, but it didn't necessarily follow that the same person was guilty of both crimes.

I pointed Fred's Jeep in the direction of the county jail. I hadn't gone far when I saw another vehicle in the distance, headed my way.

When it got close, I could see that it was a jacked-up black pickup truck with the word F O R D stretched across the hood.

I got a chill just looking at it, but it didn't swerve over into my lane and crush me as I thought it might. It simply rumbled on by, towering over my much smaller Jeep.

As it passed me by I looked up at the driver's window. Today it was rolled down, and through it I saw the unsmiling face of Deputy Norman Jackson.

▽

14

PERRY STONE LOOKED a lot worse than he had the first time I'd seen him. His face was drawn, and his hair was dirty. He kept his head down when he talked, and his voice was low. All his confidence was gone.

"They say they got the evidence on me," he said. "I don't know how they could. I never had a pistol in my truck. I don't know where it came from."

"What about your alibi?" I said. "All those friends who're going to stand up for you?"

"The Laws say they're lyin'. They say I got them to lie." He shook his head slowly, never looking up. He didn't say that his friends hadn't lied.

A few days in jail had changed him. Before, he'd looked like a man who could kill. Now, he looked like he'd been broken. Before, I would have been afraid to tell him about Brenda. Now, he looked as if the news wouldn't even register with him. He was too sunk in the misery of his current situation.

"Anybody been in to talk with you today?" I said. "Anybody who could help?"

"Brenda came in. She needs me home. I wish they'd let

me out of here so I could go and take care of her."

"Anybody come in after that?"

He still didn't look at me. "My daddy came in. He's real mad about the whole thing. Him and Mama know I didn't kill nobody, but they can't do a thing bout it."

"Nobody else? Your lawyer?"

He raised his head slowly, as if it hurt him to move it. "What do you want to know for?"

It wasn't a real show of interest, but it was better than nothing.

"It might help me to know," I said. "Something's happened that I want to find out about."

"What?"

"I don't want to tell you that," I said. "It might not even be important, and it's nothing to pin your hopes on."

"Then why do you keep askin' about who's been in to see me?"

I didn't answer him. "Just tell me who else."

"Nobody."

I was disappointed that no one but his family had been in, but maybe it was possible that Perry's father had moved the barrel. I could ask him. And of course it was also possible that someone had moved it without being told that Fred and I had been there to see it. Someone could have noticed it and decided to move it for no reason other than the fact that it was marked and therefore potentially incriminating.

I didn't have any more questions for Perry Stone, and I got up to leave.

"Wait a minute," he said as I stood. "There was somebody else, but he wasn't anybody who could help. Just the opposite, I guess. He came in right after Brenda."

I sat back down. "Who was that?" I said.

"He just wanted to ask a few questions about the pistol. I told him I'd never seen it, and that's the God's truth."

"I believe you," I said. "Did you mention what Brenda had told you?"

"I guess maybe I did. I told him she'd had a scare and that

she needed me at the house. I asked him if he thought they'd let me out. He said they wouldn't."

"And who was it that said they wouldn't?" I said.

"It was Deppidy Jackson," he said.

I went back to Fred's and gave him a report, which was unfortunately pretty skimpy.

"Too bad somebody got to that barrel," Fred said. "Not that it would've proved anything."

"It would have given us a place to start," I said. "We don't even have that, now."

"You could always go to that gas company and start talkin' to 'em about their waste disposal methods," he said.

"Sure I could. Or I could go out to Hollywood and get a job as a movie star."

"I was just kiddin'."

"Good," I said. "I don't want to take on a gas company. I don't need the grief that a big corporation can cause me. Right now, I can always go back to painting houses."

"You don't see many alligators when you have a job like that."

"Yes, and that's just one of the advantages. I also very seldom get shot at or shit on by birds."

"We've done discussed that a time or two. Didn't no birds shit on you."

"They came close."

"Close don't count."

"All right. But it was bad enough. Besides, I *did* get shot at, and someone did try to kill me with that truck."

"You say you saw Deppidy Jackson drivin' it?"

"It or one just like it. It might not have been the same one. This one had a county emblem on the driver's door. I don't know about the other one. I never got a side view of it."

Fred smiled. "Too busy runnin'," he said.

"Damn right."

He lit up a Camel. "But you still think it's the same one?"

"Has to be," I said. "I don't care if those things all look alike. When one of them tries to kill you, you remember it."

"What do you think's goin' on around here?" Fred said, blowing a smoke ring. We were standing outside by the Jeep, so the smoke ring didn't stand a chance. The wind shredded it immediately.

"Somebody's using your land for a chemical dump," I said. "Somebody killed Zach Holt and his wife. Not to mention your alligator. And somebody was making noises and calling you before all that happened. That's what's going on."

"And somebody tried to run you down in a pickup that looks like the one owned by the county."

"*Is* the one owned by the county," I said. The more I thought about it, the more certain I was.

"Okay. If you say so. And somebody moved that barrel that we saw. I know all that stuff, too. But I'm not the hot-shot detective, so what I want you to do is tell me what all that means, and who did it."

"That's the part I haven't quite worked out yet," I said.

"Which part?"

"All those parts." I hated to admit it, but it was true. "Maybe I'm not such a hot-shot detective after all."

"Don't take it too hard," Fred said, tossing the butt of the Camel to the ground and crushing it under his boot sole. "I got a lot of faith in you. It's just that this is all right puzzlin' to me."

It was puzzling to me, too. "We don't even know if all this stuff is connected," I said. "It might be a lot of separate incidents."

"What you reckon the odds would be on something like that?" Fred said.

"Pretty high, I guess."

"I'd say so."

"All right then," I said. "If it's all connected, let's try to put it together. Let's suppose Holt ran across somebody dumping the chemicals, threatened them, and got shot for his trouble."

Fred shook another Camel out of his pack. "Sounds good. So why didn't they shoot him when he found them? And why did they kill his wife? And what does all this have to do with my dead gator?"

"Holt killed the gator. He was planning to sell the skin, but he got killed before he could do it."

"Okay. So who moved the barrel?"

"Deputy Jackson. He ran across the dump, maybe because of something he found out during the Holt investigation, and took the barrel in as evidence."

"And why did he try to kill you? If it *was* him that tried to kill you, I mean?"

"I haven't got that part worked out yet."

"And what about that gun you told me about them havin', the one Perry Stone's supposed to've shot Zach with?"

"That's another little problem," I said. "It could be that Jackson is helping the gas company out. That's why he moved the barrel, tried to kill me, and framed Stone."

"It all fits, I got to admit," Fred said.

I had to admit that it fit, too. Perry had told both his father and Jackson about Brenda's seeing the lights and hearing the noise. Jackson could have gone to investigate and found the barrel, removing it to get rid of the evidence rather than to preserve it. I didn't much like Jackson, or trust him, and I could easily believe he was tied into everything.

But it still bothered me. "If it all fits," I said, "why don't I believe it?"

"Dunno. You got it all worked out."

"All except the calls and the noises."

"Yeah, well, any crank could've done those things."

"True. But why?"

"Why do cranks do anything? Just wanted to. Maybe because I wouldn't sell my land to the state for a park. Not that I've been asked. Anyway, they ought to know me better than that. Stuff like that just makes me mad. Gets my back up like an old mule's. I wouldn't sell now, even if I'd wanted to in the first place."

"I don't blame you," I said. It was nice to be a man of principle, and Fred was certainly that.

"You gonna tell the sheriff about all this?" he said.

"I guess I have to," I said.

The only thing that bothered me about talking to Sheriff Tolliver was the fear that he might tell everything I said to his chief deputy. It wasn't going to be easy to tiptoe around what I suspected and still tell most of what I knew.

I decided that the best thing to do was simply to skip over the part about my near demise under the tires of the giant truck. I could say we got suspicious about the dump for some other reason, such as the fact that I'd seen Gene Ransome head in that direction. And that had been the first reason, after all. The episode with the truck had been more frightening, but it was Ransome that had made me curious in the first place.

And that was another part of the puzzle. Ransome. I still didn't know where he fit into things. Maybe the sheriff could help with that.

The part about the gun being planted in Stone's pickup was a little more delicate, but maybe I could suggest it without being too offensive. If I planted the suspicion in just the right way, Tolliver would be very careful about what he said to Jackson, if he said anything at all.

There were still some things that bothered me, but I would just have to tell my story and see what happened.

Tolliver was in his office, tilted back in his desk chair with his sharp-pointed boots resting on the desk top. His long legs were encased in a pair of double knit Wrangler jeans, and he had on a blue-and-white-checked western-style shirt with a yoke in back. He wasn't wearing his hat, and the white streak in his hair showed to good advantage. I figured he could keep on getting elected forever, if he wanted to.

"What can I do for you, Smith?" he said, not bothering to get up or take his feet down.

He probably wouldn't have been so casual if I'd been a registered voter in the county, but since I wasn't, I didn't say anything to him about his behavior. Instead, I told him more or less what I'd planned to tell him all along.

When I finished, he did take his feet down. He put them under the desk, put his elbows on top of it, and leaned forward. "You want to make that last part a little bit more clear?" he said.

"Which part?"

"That last part. The part about the pistol that we got on Perry Stone."

"Well, Perry tells me he never had a pistol in his pickup. His wife told me that as far as she knew, he didn't own one. Maybe somebody planted it in his truck."

"That's what I thought you said. You got any idea who might've done a thing like that?"

"It could've been anybody with access to the truck," I said, hedging a bit.

He thought about it. "The truck was parked here at the jail, just waiting for us to search it. I guess a lot of people could've walked by and seen it. We didn't try to hide it."

I didn't know how far to push it, but I was afraid that if I said any more he might think I was trying to cast a bad light on his whole department, maybe even on him.

So I just said, "That makes it tough."

"Tough. Yeah. Maybe. But maybe Stone and his wife are lying and the pistol was there all the time."

I didn't believe that, and I said so.

"All right, that's your opinion. The truck was locked, though, and if you're trying to make any other kind of accusation, maybe you'd better just come right out and say it."

I wasn't ready for that kind of argument yet. "I didn't mean to imply anything," I said, feeling cowardly.

"All right, then. I'll look into things. You can be sure of that."

"What about this Gene Ransome?" I said. "He's been hanging around the county a lot, riding along on the back roads, heading down toward that dump. Do you know anything about him?"

"Not a damn thing. But I'll check him out, too. You can tell Fred Benton that I'll take care of things. Now that you've given me this information, I'll put my best man on it. If it helps us to solve the murder, so much the better." He stood up and extended his hand.

I shook with him, feeling as if he had raised me a notch in his opinion. I might not be a voter, but I was someone to reckon with.

I left the jail, wondering why I wasn't happier.

It didn't take me long to figure it out.

I wasn't happy because as far as Tolliver was concerned, Jackson was in the clear. Above suspicion. No deputy of Tolliver's could be guilty of something so crass as planting a gun behind the seat of Perry Stone's pickup. No way.

Which meant that Tolliver was going to keep right on holding Stone in jail and doing as little as possible to look for other suspects. He'd said he'd put his best man on it, but no doubt he'd simply forget it. I just hoped that he would at least see what he could find out about Gene Ransome. If Ransome was connected with Wessey Gas, then he'd have some explaining to do even if he wasn't connected with the murders.

By the time I got back to Fred's, it was time for supper. Mary had fixed chicken-fried steak with cream gravy, heavy on the black pepper. There were mashed potatoes, just in case we didn't get enough calories from the gravy and the batter on the steak, and hot buttered rolls to take care of any possible shortage if we skipped the potatoes.

I put butter on the rolls and gravy on the potatoes as well as on the steak. It wasn't often that I got to eat a home-cooked meal like that, and I wanted to take full advantage of the opportunity, even at the risk of clogging my arteries permanently within the next fifteen minutes.

Fred and I dutifully helped Mary clean off the table, but afterward we went out into the yard so Fred could smoke and not be tempted to dispose of his ashes in the sink.

"So you think Tolliver won't do much," he said after he'd lit up.

"I'm afraid he won't," I said. "He's got Stone, he's got a pistol, and he's even got a motive. If Stone can't come up with some hard proof of where he was, he might even get convicted."

"Hate to see that happen," Fred said.

He blew a smoke ring even bigger than the one that afternoon, and this one held together. The wind had died almost to nothing, and the air was warm and still. It was nearing nine o'clock, and the sun was about to sink behind the trees.

"I don't know what we can do about it," I said.

"I feel bad about that," Fred said. "I don't think the boy did it, even if that woman he's married to doesn't deserve to have him back."

I thought about Brenda. She just wanted more than a good old boy like Perry could, or would, offer her. What she saw in Zach, I'd never know, however. According to Fred, he was an outlaw who just managed to get by on the fringes of society. Having seen where he lived, I couldn't imagine that his prospects were about to improve anytime soon.

But that brought up the thought of Holt's connection with the dump. Brenda had told us he knew about it, and that it meant money in some way. How much had he known, and what did he have to do with it? I wondered if he'd known enough to get himself and his wife killed.

"If he did, Ransome's the key to the whole thing," I said aloud.

"How's that?" Fred said.

"Ransome was going to that dump to meet someone. He knows what's there, and he knows who put it there."

"You right sure about that?"

"No, but it seems likely. That's not the kind of place you'd go to on the spur of the moment. You own the land, and you don't ever visit it, but Ransome did. We've got to find him and find out what he knows."

"Well, all right. You're the detective. How do we go about doin' that?"

"I don't know. The sheriff could help us, but I don't think we can count on him. And we can't just drive around the county looking for him."

"He's got to be stayin' somewhere. Couldn't you check the motels? We don't have but two or three of 'em, so he might be pretty easy to find."

"That's as good an idea as any. I'll start tonight."

"I'll go with you," Fred said. "Always wanted to see how a real private-eye did things like that." He turned toward the house. "Let me just go in and tell Mary."

He didn't get inside, however, because that was when the noises began.

15

THE SUN HAD gone down behind the trees by then, but the sky was still light and fading into gray. It would be much darker in another fifteen minutes, but the light didn't do anything to alter the strangeness of the sounds we heard.

"That's not gators bellerin'," Fred said. "I don't know what the hell it is."

It didn't sound like anything I'd ever heard before, either. It was a sound a man could make, maybe, or an animal that was in pain. That was all I could tell. There was nothing mechanical about it.

"Is that anything like the noises you heard before?" I asked.

"Little bit, I guess," Fred said. He was straining his eyes toward the bottom land, trying to see what was making the sound. "Think we oughta go see about it?"

I thought that we should, but I didn't really want to. "Where's it coming from?"

Fred pointed. "Back down in there somewhere."

"Where the carcass is?"

"Somewhere in there. Sound does funny things back in the trees and marshes. You can't be sure."

"All right," I said. "We'll go see. But I really think we should take a gun."

"How about a rifle?"

"Right. That's what I meant. A rifle."

"I'll get one." He started for the house again, then turned back. "Mary's not gonna like this one little bit. She wouldn't let me go down there the other times."

"Tell her I'll take care of you," I said.

"That oughta do it," he said. He laughed and went in.

A few minutes later he was back, carrying a rifle and a padded leather case.

"Winchester model 94," he said. "It's a .33, holds six cartridges, and it's ready to go. It's got a lever action, so all you got to do—"

"I've fired a lever action before," I said.

"You don't have to act like you got your feelin's hurt. I just wanted to be sure. Safety's right here." He put the rifle in the case, zipped it, and put the case in the back of the Jeep. "I got some more cartridges in my pocket, in case we need 'em. I hope we don't."

"Probably won't," I said. "But I've been shot at and chased by a man-eating truck lately. This time I want to be able to fight back. And if a blond woman tries to hold me at gunpoint with a .22—excuse me, I mean at *rifle*point—then I want something to shoot her with."

We climbed into the Jeep and Fred started it up. "You wouldn't really shoot a woman, would you?" he said.

"The way I feel right now? Sure I would."

Fred shook his head. He was a real old-time Texan, full of respect and reverence for women, even if they were holding a rifle on him. At least in theory he was. I decided not to remind him of some of the things he'd said about Brenda last night.

The noises had stopped by the time Fred went into the house, and I hadn't heard them again. Bouncing around in the Jeep, I would have had a hard time hearing anything.

When we got down to the gator carcass, Fred stopped. It was fully dark, and over the ticking sound of the cooling engine I could hear insects humming and splashes in the water. A mosquito buzzed around my head.

"Did you ever see that old movie called *Alligator People*?"

"I don't think I ever heard of that one," Fred said, leaning on the steering wheel. He doused the lights, and we were sitting in deep blackness. "Who was in it?"

"Lon Chaney, Junior, I think. He played a man with a hook instead of a hand on one arm."

"You watch that kind of thing much?"

"Not too often. It was on late at night once when I didn't feel like changing the channel."

"Who were these alligator people?"

"I don't know," I said. "Victims of some crazy doctor's crazy experiments, I think."

"How come you think about somethin' like that right now?" he said.

"I don't know. Just the general atmosphere around here, I guess. You hear any more of those noises?"

We both sat and listened. A bullfrog croaked. The mosquitoes hummed. Nothing else.

"Maybe we oughta go on back to the house," Fred said.

He was probably right, and we might have gone if we hadn't heard the noise again. It sounded more like a man who'd been kicked in the belly by a horse than anything.

"It's farther off now," Fred said. "You want to go see about it?"

"No," I said. "But I think we should, anyway. Just don't forget the rifle, and don't say anything like, 'You check over there, and I'll look down this way.' "

"What's that mean?"

"That's what they always say in movies like *Alligator People* right before someone gets hurt or killed. We don't want to get separated."

"You don't have to worry about that," Fred said. "I'll stick to you like a burr to a cat's tail." He started the Jeep. "Jeep won't go much farther, though. We're gonna have to get out and walk in a minute."

We drove for about another quarter of a mile, and then

the marshes and the trees put an end to the driving.

"I could prob'ly go just about anywhere in this Jeep," Fred said. "But it's too damn dark to take any chances. I don't want to puncture a tire or sink in over the axles. Even the Jeep won't pull out of a mess like that."

We got out and he retrieved the rifle, along with the flashlight we had used the previous night.

"Which way?" I said.

"I'd say straight ahead." He pointed with the light. "Like I said, it's hard to tell about sounds, but that's the way that would lead us over to where that dump was. Seems right to me that we'd find out where the sound's comin' from if we went that way."

I shrugged. "All right, why not? What's between us and the dump?"

He started walking, and I followed closely. "There's another big lake, biggest one on my property, but we'll skirt around the end of it. Have to go through some pretty marshy ground, but it ought to be solid enough to hold us. No quicksand, I hope."

"I hope so too," I said, fighting the urge to stop right there.

"Lots of dead trees," he said. "The ones that haven't fallen down yet. Don't know what happened. Some kinda blight. After that, some higher ground with lots of trees. Then some more marsh, and then the dump."

"How far is all that?"

"Mile or two."

What was a mile to an old runner like me? At least my knee was still holding up after my adventure with the truck. A good walk shouldn't bother it.

The night had gotten cloudy, and the darkness seemed almost like a solid presence. The humidity had come back and made the illusion of solidity even more real. I knew that we should be watching ourselves and keeping an eye out for whatever had made the noise, but it was all we could do to find a path over the marshy ground.

I thought I could see the shallow end of the lake, but I

wasn't sure. The dark ground became the dark water, and it was hard to tell which one was which. Our feet occasionally sank into mud, and we pulled them out with a sucking sound.

"Should've brought our rubber boots," Fred said.

"I don't have any," I told him.

"Don't matter, then," he said.

Then I could see the dead trees sticking up on our right. They looked ghostly and pale in the darkness, as if there were something in their skeletons that gave off a faint glow. New growth, mostly thick bushes, had sprung up around them. The bushes were probably green, but they looked black in the darkness, like amorphous blobs gathered around the bases of the trees.

Fred stopped suddenly. "You hear somethin'?" he said.

"Nothing but bugs and frogs," I said. "I thought I heard an owl a minute ago, though."

"That ain't what I heard."

He stood there, sweeping the beam of the flashlight around. It passed over the bushes, which were green, all right, and over the branches of the dead trees, across the ground in front of us and out over the shallow water, which I could now recognize by the reflection of the light. I thought I caught sight of a pair of red eyes in the beam's passing, but I couldn't be sure.

"I don't see anything," I said.

"Me neither, but it don't mean there's nothin' there." He kept playing the light around.

"What did you hear?" I said.

"Don't know. Just a noise, but it didn't sound natural."

"Maybe it was nothing," I said.

"It was somethin', all right," he said, but after a minute or so of looking we still hadn't seen anything unusual.

"I guess I'm gettin' old," Fred said. "Let's go."

We started forward, but we got only about twenty feet before we both stopped. This time, I'd heard it too, the sound of metal on metal, a faint click that sounded as out of place in this setting as a violin solo would have.

"The bushes," I said, and Fred shined the light over on them.

We still saw nothing unusual. There were just thick green bushes and dead white trees.

"We're missing something somewhere," I said. "Shine the light down a little lower."

This time, Fred put the light on the ground and we saw something immediately. Tire tracks, wide gouges in the earth that made deep ruts running back to the bushes.

I thought of a vehicle I'd had a recent encounter with, one whose tires were high and wide.

Then the bushes exploded, flying in all directions, or that's the way it looked to me at the time.

I suppose that first there was the sound of the truck's starter, and the noise of the rear tires spinning to find a grip in the mud, or maybe all those things happened at the same time. What I remember, though, is those bushes flying through the air and that black truck bearing down on us with Fred just standing there holding the flashlight right on it and those silver letters, F O R D, shining in the light. Then the truck went through a puddle, and water flew up around those wide tires, catching the light beam and showering down like drops of gold.

About then my brain kicked back into gear.

"Get out of the way!" I yelled, throwing myself to one side and hoping Fred would do the same.

He was old, but he was quick. And the truck was far enough away to give him time.

He dropped the flashlight, though, and it lay on the ground, its beam still glowing but not helping a thing.

The truck swerved in my direction, and I got off my hands and knees, covered with mud and slime.

"Shoot!" I yelled to Fred. "Shoot!"

I had already gone through this bit with the truck once too often to suit me, and a silly scene from another movie popped into my head. I could see Peter Falk and Alan Arkin in *The In-Laws* and hear Falk telling Arkin to "Serpentine!"

Maybe that wasn't such a bad idea. I gave it a try.

I could hear the truck behind me, slurping through the mud, trying to get a bead on me. I was headed in the wrong direction, toward the lake, but I didn't want to turn back.

I heard the crack of Fred's rifle, but I heard no impact from the bullet. It was no wonder. Fred was shooting under almost impossible conditions.

Then I had a sobering thought. Now they knew who had the rifle. Whoever it was might go after Fred, but certainly not until I was out of the way. After all, I was practically helpless.

On the other hand, I found myself already sloshing around in water up over my ankles, and the truck behind me, while very tall, wasn't amphibious. If I could get out into deep water, I might have a chance.

The water would have to be very deep, though. I had a feeling that the driver of the truck would push it as far as he could.

When the water was up to my calves, the truck was only a few yards away. My shadow fled in front of me, and I felt like a rabbit spotlighted by an illegal hunter.

There were a couple more rifle cracks behind me, Fred shooting at the truck. I don't think he hit it.

Thick lily-pad vines were wrapping themselves round my legs. I did a flat dive and tried swimming under the water. It was barely deep enough, but I thought I was covered. I swam straight ahead for about fifteen feet, then struck out at an angle to the left, trying to get out of the truck's path.

When I came up for air, the truck had stopped. My little move had misled the driver, and the headlights were not pointing in my direction. I ducked back under and swam toward the truck. I had in mind a sneak attack, but it didn't work out exactly as I had planned.

I surfaced on the passenger side just as the door was closing. Someone had gotten out and dropped down into the water with me.

The truck began to back up.

The man in the water was just a dark shape and the driver of the truck cut the wheels the wrong way, so that the headlight beams were pointing away from us. I slid back under the water and went for the shape's legs.

He probably thought an alligator had him. I know that's what I would have thought.

He tried stomping and kicking, and even in the roiling mud and water I could hear him yelling. I held on and got a good grip, trying to bring him down.

When he splashed into the water, I tried to get to his arms and pin them, but it was like fighting a windmill. He was churning the water, kicking and yelling as if he were in a battle to the death with a prehistoric monster. His fear must have been pumping adrenaline into his system by the quart.

Something splashed into the water not far from us, a serious splash, not the kind a frog could make even if he were the champion bullfrog of the year. There was something really big there.

I gave up trying to subdue the man and simply tried to pull him away, but I couldn't get a grip. He was thrashing around so much that there was nothing to hold, or at least nothing that would stay still long enough for me to get a grip on.

There was another huge splash nearby, and I saw the dark head of a gator, its jaws wide, break the water.

I was suddenly as scared as the man thrashing in the water, maybe even more scared. I wanted out of there, but I wanted to get the man out too. There were a lot of things I wanted to ask him.

I made one more grab and got hold of his belt. I started backing up as fast as I could, pulling him after me. The going was hard, and my ankle tangled in a lily-pad stem. I fell back into the water, losing my hold on the belt.

When I got up and dashed the water out of my eyes, the man was screaming. The gator had been luckier than I had been and had managed to get a grip on his arm. I could see the dark head, the jaws clamped shut.

I found the belt and pulled again.

The gator pulled back. He was a lot stronger than I was. I was afraid that if I didn't let go, the man's arm would be chewed off. But if I did let go, the gator would drag the man away from me.

I pulled again, but it was no use. The belt slipped out of my hands, and the man slid across the water, screaming.

I stood there watching as he slipped below the surface of the lake, the screams abruptly changing to burbling and then being cut off altogether.

It was only then that I could hear the roaring of the truck engine and another rifle shot.

Well, hell, I thought. What was I supposed to do now?

One thing was for sure, and that was that I didn't owe the guy in the water a single thing. He hadn't gotten out of the truck to give me a good citizenship award, and Fred was my client, after all.

Still, Fred could take care of himself pretty well, and he had the gun. Or the rifle.

And I got a sick feeling deep down in my stomach when I thought about the man's arm in the alligator's mouth. He had been scared to begin with, and he must have wanted to stay in the truck. But whoever was in there had forced him out, and the instant I had wrapped my arms around his legs he had gone into a complete panic. The sheer terror he must have felt when the gator latched onto his arm was almost more than I could even begin to imagine.

So naturally I had to go after him to try to do something for him, as hopeless as it seemed. I knew he would never have done the same for me, no matter who he was, but that didn't seem to matter.

I blundered forward in the water toward the spot where I thought he'd gone under. It was so dark that all the spots looked pretty much alike, black water covered by the darker circles of the lily pads. I fought my way through them, feeling in front of me with my outstretched arms, cold chills racing over me at the thought that one of them might wind up in those horrible teeth, which I thought I remembered from my reading were not made for chewing at all but for ripping and shredding.

Didn't gators drown their food, carry it off somewhere to rot and then swallow it whole before digesting it?

It was a disgusting thought, and when my arms rammed into a solid object, I jumped straight up out of the water.

It was the body of the man, lying quite still now.

I got the belt in my hand and pulled backward.

There was no resistance, and then the water boiled beside him and two gators exploded to the surface, thrashing the water to a silver froth around me. It was almost as if they were standing on their tails, and they had something in their mouths that they were fighting over, shaking their heads from side to side like dogs fighting over a bone.

It wasn't a bone. It was an arm, or what was left of one— not much more than a bone at that, most likely.

I tugged on the body with all my strength, moving backward with more speed than I would have thought possible, as the thrashing gators sank back under the water, which heaved around them as if others had come to join the fun and games.

In no time at all I was in the shallow water, and I could see the blood streaming out of the stump of the man's arm, leaving a black trail on the ripples. I knew that I had no time to stop and render aid. If I didn't get out of there at once, the blood might call up all the monsters of the deep, and even those that were fighting might decide that it would be more profitable to come after us than to continue chewing over a bare bone.

Finally I got to relatively dry ground, and hoping that I was far enough from danger, I tried to staunch the bleeding. I ripped off the man's belt and wrapped it as tightly around the stump of his arm as I could. There wasn't much room to operate. The arm was gone a few inches below the shoulder, and shreds of flesh and cloth hung loosely and wetly there.

When my heart had slowed down to about twice normal,

the blood stopped rushing in my ears and I could hear more or less as usual again. Except for my ragged breathing and the splashing of the agitated gators, who apparently enjoyed a good fight among themselves, I couldn't hear a thing.

There was no sound of the truck, no sound of rifle fire, no sound at all.

I propped the man against a strong tuft of cattails and looked around. I could make out the trees standing there as dead as ever, their stark branches outlined against the black sky, but there was no sign of the truck and there was no sign of Fred.

$\triangledown$

16

I KEPT LOOKING from side to side until at last I saw the faint glow of the flashlight. I walked over to where it had been mashed into the soft ground by one of the tires on the truck. Being made of nearly indestructible plastic, it was still burning.

"That you, Truman?" Fred called from somewhere when I pulled the light from the mud.

"It's me," I said, looking around for him.

Off to my left the bushes began to shake, and Fred emerged from them carrying his rifle.

"Son of a bitch got away," he said. "Hell, it's only because I'm so damn old and slow. And I can't see worth a damn anymore, either."

His night vision was better than mine, but I didn't remind him.

"I got off six shots," he said. "Missed ever' damn time, I think. He was comin' right at me on two of 'em, and I missed anyhow. Then I couldn't get the shells out of my pocket and load the rifle, so I had to duck back into those bushes and hide. He thrashed 'em pretty good with that truck, but he didn't have a chance of findin' me." He paused for breath. "What happened to you?"

"I ran into the lake," I said. "He didn't get me, either, but he sent somebody after me."

"Who was it?"

"I don't know," I said. "Now that we've got the flashlight, why don't we go over there and take a look?'

I told Fred what had happened so that he wouldn't be too shocked at the sight of the arm, but the thought of it didn't bother him at all.

"Son of a bitch got what he deserved," was the way he put it, and I had to agree with him, though I still felt sorry for the man.

I was a little disoriented, and it took us a few minutes to find where I'd left him. When we got there I shined the light into his face.

It was Gene Ransome, and the light didn't bother him at all. He stared right into it with wide-open eyes. His low-growing hair was plastered to his forehead, and his mouth hung open.

He was as dead as the ghostly trees that stood behind us. The shock of the gator's attack and the loss of his arm and so much blood had been too much for him.

I told Fred who he was.

"I guess we'll find out now for sure who he is and who he's workin' for," Fred said. "Damn, I hate to have to drive that Jeep in here after him in the dark."

"We can leave him till morning," I said. "He won't mind a bit."

"Yeah, but there might not be much of him left by then, not if those gators come after him."

I hadn't thought of that. "You think that's likely?" I said.

"Could be. You can't predict 'em. Hell, you don't ever know what might be back in those trees and bushes. 'Coons might get at him. Turtles. Who knows what-all."

"I guess we should try to get him out of here then," I said. "You go get the Jeep. I'll stay here and keep everything off him until you get back."

"Hardly seems worth the trouble, somehow," Fred said,

looking down at the dead man and shaking his head.

"We might need him for evidence," I said. "We want proof of what happened here tonight."

"All right, but I'm gonna need the flashlight. And if I sink down to China in that Jeep, you're gonna be here by yourself all night."

"I'll just have to chance it," I said, but I didn't like the thought of being alone with the body for any length of time. I thought I might be able to fight off a turtle, if it was a small one, but I wasn't too keen on the idea of fighting off an alligator.

"You can keep the rifle, though," Fred said. "I don't think whoever was in that truck will be after me. He headed off the other way."

Fred handed me the rifle and dug in his pocket for the extra cartridges. "Here," he said, handing them to me. "You better load that thing."

Having the rifle would be better than nothing. "Where do you shoot an alligator?" I said.

"Hell, I never shot one. In the eye, I guess. That way you won't ruin the skin. But I sure hope you don't have to shoot one. That's what you came here for in the first place, to find out who killed my gator."

It seemed like a long time ago. "I remember," I said. "I'll try to restrain myself."

"Well, if you have to, you have to. Better him than you. Don't worry about it." He started walking in the direction of the Jeep.

I watched him go and thought about what a mess we were in. Now we had another corpse, and we still didn't know who was to blame. It was easy to see that it wasn't Perry Stone, however, and considering the vehicle involved, I thought I knew who to look for.

Everything fit, and there was the additional consideration that whoever was dumping the PCBs, or whatever they were dumping, nearly had to have the cooperation of the local law.

Jackson, being in charge of the rustling investigation,

could easily steer things the way he wanted them to go and keep suspicion away from the real reason there were trucks on the county roads at night. Sheriff Tolliver was unfortunately blind to the possibility that one of his own men could be involved in something illegal, and that was an obstacle I'd have to overcome. After what had happened tonight, I thought it might be a little easier.

I thought for a while about who had told what to whom. The thing that worried me was that Brenda had told Perry about the noises, though she had been one of the people making them. Perry had told Jackson.

But why had Brenda told Perry? Because she wanted to cover her own tracks in case someone told him that she had been down there? Or did she have another reason? Her quick anger still bothered me.

Before long, I felt like a newspaper reporter writing a story about President Reagan and the Iran-contra scandal. What did he know, and when did he know it?

Then I heard the Jeep and saw its lights. At that instant something that I should have thought of before hit me dead between the eyes. I turned it over in my mind and looked at it carefully. It explained everything I'd thought of before and one thing I hadn't, a thing I should have considered.

Fred drove up and got out. "Thought a time or two I wouldn't make it," he said. "But here I am. Let's see if we can get your friend in the Jeep."

We did, but it wasn't easy. "Dead weight" is more than just an expression.

"You have any visitors?" Fred said when we had Ransome stowed behind the seats.

"Not a one," I said.

I had been so busy thinking about the tangle of events that an entire herd of alligators, or whatever a group of gators was called, could have come up to steal Ransome away from me and I would never have noticed them.

"How far from that dump are we?" I said.

"You thinkin' about goin' over there?"

"You got this far."

"Yeah," he said. "But I'd already walked over the ground. I kind of knew where to drive, and I still nearly lost it a couple of times."

"We could walk," I said. "Nothing's going to take Ransome out of the back of the Jeep."

"I guess we could," he said. "We're nearly there. But what for?"

"To see if there's anyone there. Maybe the truck is there waiting for us. Maybe the driver didn't leave."

"You load that rifle?"

"Yes," I said.

"All right, then. I guess you better be the one to carry it. Maybe you can do better with it than I did."

I wasn't so sure about that, but I didn't argue. "Which way?" I said.

Fred pointed the flashlight beam. "That way."

We started walking.

"These sure are good batteries in this flashlight," Fred said. "I never could figure out why they named them for that baseball player, though."

"What baseball player?" I said.

"He might've been before your time. Played for Detroit back in the fifties. If he'd been around now, he'd be making millions, though. He was better than ninety-nine percent of those fellas you see today. Maybe that's why they named the batteries for him, because he was so good and so dependable."

"Who are you talking about?" I said.

"Al Kaline," Fred said.

I walked along for a few steps without saying anything. Fred had never told me a joke before, and I didn't know for sure whether he was telling me one now. For all I knew, he was serious.

We walked along for a few steps, and Fred started to laugh. "I got you on that one," he said.

He had, so I laughed too. "How much farther?" I said.

"Not far. If an old fart like me can make it, you can make it too."

I had to admit that he was in pretty good shape for an old fart. I said so.

"It's not that I don't hurt in the mornin's," he said. "I think when you get to be my age, you hurt in the mornin' no matter what you do. So I just keep goin' along. It hurts to get out of a rockin' chair, too, so why not get some exercise?"

We followed the beam of the flashlight as it threw shadows along in front of us. I asked Fred how he thought the dumping might have gotten started.

"Hard to say. I told you that I never come back in here—you can see why. The gators down in there are mean, and it's hard travelin'. I could go around, I guess, the way we got in the other night, but I just never thought about it. I like for things to be wild, and I guess I must've thought of this part of the land back in here as a little bit like a jungle, like somethin' I was lettin' go back to nature without any interference from me or anybody else."

He walked for a while without saying more. I didn't prod him.

"Maybe it was a bad idea," he said finally. "I should've checked up on things, but I never thought of it. Who'd think anybody would just go through the fence and dump stuff on my place?"

"Somebody thought of it," I said.

"Yeah, they did, didn't they? Had to be somebody that knew the area, though."

I asked who that might be.

"Hell, it could be anybody from around here. You don't have to be too smart to find the place."

"What about the Stones?"

"Sure, they would've known about it. Why? You think they're in on this?"

"Not really," I said. "I think I've got things about figured out now. Not everything, maybe, but most of it."

"That's good. You gonna tell me, or just keep me in suspense?"

"I'll tell you later," I said. "When all the loose ends are tied up."

"Loose ends?"

"I still don't know who killed your alligator," I said.

"Damn. That's the thing I really wanted to know."

He might have pursued the topic, but we had gotten close to the area where the dumping had been going on.

"This is about it," Fred said.

"Turn off the light," I said, whispering.

He clicked off the beam and darkness settled around us. We stood there letting our eyes get used to it.

"What do you think we're gonna find here?"

"I don't know. I know you said the truck came this way, so maybe it's still around."

We stood there quietly, listening. I could hear muffled noises through the trees.

"How much farther to where we were last night?" I said.

"Quarter of a mile, maybe."

"Think we can walk it in the dark?"

"If we're careful. Slide your feet along, sort of, don't trip, and watch out for limbs in your face."

"All right," I said. "We won't talk anymore. I'll tap you on the shoulder if I want to stop. You do the same for me."

"Right."

We started out, and I felt a little bit like Daniel Boone. Or at least an imitation of him. I needed a coonskin cap. Or was that Davy Crockett? It didn't matter. They were both Fess Parker.

We moved slowly now, but as we got closer to the spot, the noises became clearer. When we were nearly there, I could distinguish voices. I tapped Fred on the shoulder.

"How many more we got?" someone said. He had a hoarse voice.

"Ten more," a man answerd. "We got to bury them, too."

"Shit, I hate that. Why can't we just dump 'em in the water?"

"They said not to. Somebody did that once, and they got their ass canned for it. We won't be bringing any more stuff out here after tonight."

"Fine by me," the hoarse voice said. "These goddamn mosquitoes are about to chew my ass off."

I wish he hadn't mentioned the mosquitoes. When we were walking, a couple had buzzed by my face, but they hadn't bothered me. Now I could hear them and feel them all over me. Most of it was probably my imagination, but some of it certainly wasn't. I resisted the urge to slap a stinging area of my neck.

I heard a barrel being tilted on its side and rolled to the back of a truck. I heard a grunt as someone took it and eased it down.

I had hoped to find the black pickup, but this was much better—positive proof of what had been happening here. All we had to do was get these two men to the jail, or to a good district attorney, and we had our case made. And I was the one with the rifle.

I tapped Fred again and we started forward, with me in the lead. When we stepped into the clearing, I pointed the rifle at the man on the ground. He was rolling a barrel over to join a number of others.

"That looks like a good place to rest," I said.

"What the hell," the man said. He was the one with the hoarse voice. I couldn't see him too well in the darkness, but he was big enough to make a nice target.

I turned to the truck. "Why don't you jump down and join your friend?" I said.

The man in the truck didn't hesitate. Fred had turned the flashlight on him, and maybe he could see a little of the beam glint on the rifle barrel. He jumped down and walked over to his friend.

They stood together in the light, unsure of what to do.

They were both big, wearing jeans and T-shirts that were grimy with dirt and sweat.

"This is private property, you know," I said.

"*My* private property," Fred said. "I could shoot the both of you right here and leave you for the buzzards, and nobody would give a damn."

I didn't know the law on that point, but it sounded impressive. "You want the rifle?" I said.

"Hell, you shoot 'em, and I'll say I done it," Fred said. "I don't need the rifle."

"Hold on just a damn minute," the hoarse one said. "We're just a couple of guys doing a job. Work's hard to come by these days. We didn't know this was your land."

"You must've known it was somebody's," Fred said.

"Hey, we just do what we're hired to do. That's my truck." He pointed to the bobtail that his buddy had jumped out of. "I do a lot of haulin'. Fella just gives me the load, tells me where to haul it, and I carry it off. Unload and go home. That's my job. That's all I know."

"Not a very curious guy, are you?" I said.

"Hell, no. I need the money."

"Bad enough to risk prison?"

"Shit. Prison? For just trespassin'? You gotta be kiddin'."

"Yeah," said a voice behind me. "You gotta be kiddin'."

It was Deputy Jackson.

17

JACKSON WAS HOLDING a flashlight in one hand, but it wasn't on. In the other he was holding a short-barreled pistol. He wasn't pointing the pistol at anyone in particular; he didn't even seem to be gripping it very tightly. It was just there in his hand, ready to be used for whatever he wanted it to be used for.

"What's this about trespassin'?" he said.

"Glad you're here, Deppidy," Fred said. "These men are on my land without my permission, and it looks to me like they're dumpin' stuff out here. We weren't really gonna shoot 'em, but I guess I got a right to do that."

"Depends," Jackson said, walking over closer to us.

The two men from the truck hadn't said anything, and it didn't appear that they intended to. I kept the rifle on them and tried to watch Jackson at the same time. It wasn't easy.

"I sure don't like people who have a way of turnin' up in awkward situations like this, Smith," Jackson said. "Seems like the last time we met, it was at the scene of a murder. Now here we are again, and you've got two men covered with a rifle. You're beginnin' to seem like a real dangerous man."

I tried to see what he was doing with the pistol. "I'm not

very dangerous," I said. "Were Holt and his wife killed with a rifle?"

"I wouldn't know about that. What I do know is that I told you I didn't like you and didn't want you messin' around in my business."

"Is this your business?" I said.

"You're damn right it's my business. Law enforcement in this county is my business, not the business of some outsider like you."

"Just a damn minute here," Fred said. "Seems to me like there's a lot of stuff goin' on in this county that you law enforcement folks aren't gettin' much done about, not even countin' my dead gator. For one thing, it looks to me like this dumpin' has been goin' on for a good while."

"Maybe it has," Jackson said. "That's not my fault." He looked at the two men I was covering with the rifle. "Why don't you two fellas go sit on the back end of your truck."

The men walked over to the truck and climbed up on the back end and sat there. I followed them with the rifle, but they didn't seem worried at all. In fact, they were looking almost cheerful.

Fred noticed their chipper attitude. "What're those two lookin' so smug for? You'd think that with the law here, they'd be scared spitless, knowin' that they were headed for jail quicker'n Jack could skin a rabbit."

"Maybe they're just two law-abiding citizens, doing their job," I said.

"That's right," the hoarse one said. "Just two fellas doin' a job of work, tryin' to make an honest dollar."

"Or maybe they think they've got friends in the right places," I said, trying to watch Jackson out of the corner of my eye.

"What do you mean by that?" Jackson said, his voice cold.

"Oh, hell," Fred said. "Let's don't pussyfoot around it any more. He means that somebody has tried twice to run him down in that jacked-up county truck, once just a little while ago. Tried to get me, too, that time, but we got away."

"So?" Jackson said.

"So who the hell do you think was drivin' that truck?" Fred said.

Jackson didn't move or answer. He just stood there, very still, looking at the two men sitting in the bobtail, dangling their feet as if they didn't have a worry in the world. Maybe they didn't.

"Goddammit," Fred said. "Why didn't you dig a bullet out of that dead gator of mine?"

Jackson turned his head slightly to look at Fred. "I thought about it. It just seemed like a messy job that might not pan out." His voice had an apologetic sound, as if he were a bit embarrassed at his own squeamishness.

The hoarse man laughed. Jackson didn't tell him to stop.

"There are a few other things, too," I said. "Like that pistol you found in Perry Stone's truck, the one that Stone swears he didn't put there. He said he never even owned a pistol like that."

"It was there when I looked," Jackson said, no longer apologetic. He wasn't looking for an argument.

That was fine with me. I wasn't going to give him one. Not about the pistol.

"There's the rustling, too," I said. "You were the one who was supposed to be investigating that, except that there wasn't any rustling going on. The trucks that people heard at night, they were all coming to the same place. Right here. Nobody was missing any cattle, but somehow the rustling story got all over the county. And the rustlers never got caught."

"They're caught now," Fred said. "But it turns out that they ain't rustlers."

"And you beat up Perry Stone," I told Jackson.

"He started that fight," Jackson said. "Not me."

"You were out to get him from the very beginning. You kept him in jail even though he had witnesses to say he wasn't around Holt's place on the day of the murders."

"They were lyin'," Jackson said. "It was three people, all

speakin' up for the other. Not one of 'em had an independent witness to say Perry was with 'em."

"Still, you went after him pretty quick."

"He'd had trouble with Holt before."

"It all sounds pretty simple, doesn't it?" I said. "But it's not that simple, and you know it."

"What is it that I know?" he said. He sounded genuinely curious.

"You know the clincher. This dumping couldn't be going on without help from the law. There's not a way in the world these men could have gotten away with this if they hadn't paid someone off."

"I knew I didn't like you, Smith," he said.

"What about me?" Fred said. "You like me? I'll back up ever'thing he's sayin'."

"I guess I don't like you much, either, then," Jackson said.

"Then I don't give a damn," Fred said. "Trouble is, it's all the truth. And it all seems to me to point right at one man."

Fred hesitated a second, knowing that Jackson had the pistol and I had the rifle, which probably wouldn't be as quick if we needed it.

Then he said, "At you, is where it seems to me to be pointing."

Jackson stood there looking at the two men in the truck, who looked back at him through the darkness. He didn't say anything to them or to Fred, however.

"I think you might be wrong, Fred," I said.

"Wrong? How in the hell could I be wrong? Look at those two assholes over there, lookin' like they just won the damn lottery. Why don't he take 'em in if he's not in on it with 'em?"

"He's thinking about it," I said.

"What the hell's he got to think about?"

"A lot," I said. "If he didn't frame Stone, who did? If he's supposed—"

"—to be investigating the rustling, why didn't anybody tell him?" a voice finished for me.

"Hello, Sheriff," I said.

Tolliver came walking from around the side of the bobtail. The two men sitting in it didn't seem at all surprised to see him.

"I thought you might be coming by," I said.

"Actually, I never left," he said. "I was just waiting to see what developed."

"The truck must be around in front of the bobtail," I said.

"Yeah, that's where it is. You're a slippery bastard, Smith. How'd you get away from Ransome?"

"It was easy," I said. "He was scared half to death. The alligators accounted for the other half."

"That silly son of a bitch," Tolliver said. "He was so scared he was almost pissing his pants."

"He had a right to be scared," I said. "All his worst fears came true."

"That's too bad," Tolliver said. "You can pitch that rifle down, by the way. And I guess you might as well throw that pistol over here by me, Jackson."

I thought for a second or two that Jackson might make a play. If he had, I might have tried something myself, but neither of us did anything. I dropped the rifle, and Jackson tossed the pistol into the mud near Tolliver.

"Pick that thing up, will you, Lonnie?" Tolliver said.

The hoarse man hopped down and picked up the pistol.

"I sure as to God wish I knew what in the everlovin' hell was goin' on here," Fred said.

"I can tell you that," I said. "Remember when we were talking about how the dumpers needed the cooperation of the law? And we thought it was Jackson who was cooperating? Well, we were wrong. It was the big man himself."

"How long have you known?" Tolliver said.

"Not long," I told him. "In fact, it just came to me back there when the alligators were dining on your buddy Ransome."

"I sure wish you'd told me," Fred said.

"I wasn't sure. And then Deputy Jackson showed up here

with his pistol in his hand, and I thought maybe we'd been right all along. It was a little confusing."

"Jackson's been doing a little poking around all on his own," the sheriff said. "Looks like he's found out more than he should have, too, but just a little too late."

"I just wish I'd caught on to you a little sooner," Jackson said. "People kept askin' me about the rustlin', like I was supposed to know. I finally remembered who'd told me about it in the first place. And then I heard that I was the one who was supposed to be in charge of the case. It made me wonder a little bit."

"Then there was that pistol in Stone's truck," I said.

"Yeah. I asked him over and over, but he kept on sayin' that it couldn't be his. And that pickup had been at the jail a whole day before the sheriff told me to search it. If anybody put that pistol there, it was him."

"I'm not admitting a thing," Tolliver said, sounding smug. "I would like to know, though, what it was that got you onto me, Smith."

"It took me a while to realize that everything pointing to Jackson could point to you just as well. I'm sure he's not the only one with the keys to the county's truck."

"There's gotta be more to it than that," Tolliver said. He was probably wondering whether anyone else was going to figure out just what had been happening.

"Not much," I said. "The main thing was how much you protested today when I hinted that Jackson might have planted that pistol. You didn't want that getting out, because Jackson might think of you. It turns out that he already had."

"Hell, nobody'd believe you thought of me just because of that."

"Maybe not, but along with everything else, it adds up. And then there was the clincher. After I told you all I knew this afternoon, the funny noises started again. Somebody wanted to get me and Fred down in the woods to do us in. Who knew I was getting too close? Jackson? He'd chased me off from around here once, if it was him, but that's all. If it was you, though, that plus everything I told you added up to big trouble if I put it all together." I shook my head. "I did, but it was a little too late."

"Don't blame yourself, son," Fred said. "Hell, ever'body thought the sheriff was an honest man."

"They must have offered you a lot of money," I said.

"Enough," Tolliver said. "So the only problem is, what do we do with you now?"

"Shoot 'em and dump 'em in a hole with the barrels. Cover 'em up and leave 'em there," Lonnie said.

Fred had been exaggerating when he had suggested that we shoot the men for trespassing, but this was different. This time, no one was kidding.

"That's a lot of bodies to leave lying around," I said. "Four, counting Ransome."

"If you're telling the truth about him there's not much left to lie around," Tolliver said. "And that's a good idea for all of you. Tie 'em up, Merle."

Lonnie's buddy jumped off the back of the bobtail "Where's the rope?" he said.

"Back of my truck," Tolliver said, and Merle walked off to get it.

"You three can sit down," Tolliver said. "Lonnie, get me that rifle."

Lonnie came over and got the rifle, and we sat down. There wasn't much else to do.

In a minute, Merle came back with some nylon rope.

"Tie their hands and feet," Tolliver said, and Merle proceeded to do a very efficient job.

I wanted to say something, to tell Tolliver that he couldn't do this to us, but I'd heard that line in too many bad movies.

Besides, he very obviously *could* do this to us.

"Put 'em in the back of my truck," Tolliver said.

Merle and Lonnie picked Fred up like he was a sack of feed and hauled him off. Then they came for Jackson.

By the time they came back for me, there was hardly any feeling at all left in my hands. Merle tied a mean knot.

They carried me to the truck, one holding my shoulders and the other my feet. I tried to sag on them, to go limp, to give them as much trouble as dead weight could. It didn't help. They tossed me high in the air and over into the back of the truck. I never thought they could do it, but moving all those barrels must have given them some real muscle.

I landed on Fred and Jackson. It wasn't that they wanted to break my fall. They were just in the way.

I heard the air go out of Fred.

"Sorry about that," I said.

He sucked in a deep breath, but he didn't try to say anything.

"How is it they do things in the movies?" I said. "Don't we put our backs to each other and work on the knots?"

"Might as well try it," Jackson said. "I don't expect it'll work."

His pessimism was justified. I couldn't even feel his hands, much less the knots.

"I can't feel yours, either," he said.

That was when I knew we were in real trouble.

Lonnie climbed up in the truck bed with us. Merle and Tolliver got up in the cab. The doors slammed, and we were off to visit the gators. They probably had their appetites stimulated by Ransome and were really eager for more.

For some reason I thought about the crocodile in *Peter Pan*, the one who got a taste of Captain Hook and followed him forever after, hoping for another. I wondered if alligators and crocodiles were alike that way.

"You fellas gonna be a mighty good meal," Lonnie said as we jounced along. He was standing braced against the back of the cab, holding Jackson's pistol.

We didn't answer him. It's hard to talk when you're lying facedown in a truck bed with your hands and feet tied, especially when you're being bounced around by the motion of the truck.

I wondered if Tolliver would really throw us to the gators. I wondered if he'd kill us first.

I wondered if Dino would keep on feeding Nameless if I never came back.

Then the truck stopped.

Lonnie stepped over us and opened the tailgate. He didn't mess around with us after that, just slid us over the steel bed and out onto the ground.

It was quite a fall, but the ground was soft. The breath went out of me for a second, but I didn't think anything was broken, not that it was going to matter very much in a little while.

Tolliver and Merle were standing over us. Lonnie looked down from the truck bed.

"I just wanta know one thing," Fred said. He had landed facedown in the mud, but he had managed to roll over so that he could talk.

"What's that?" Tolliver said.

"Are you the son of a bitch that killed my gator?"

$\triangledown$

18

I WANTED TO laugh, but that's not easy to do when you've got a mouthful of dirt—cold, damp, and gritty. I spit most of it out and ran my tongue around my teeth trying to clear the rest of it. There were a few grass blades in there, too.

Tolliver laughed loud enough for both of us, anyway. "Hell, old man, you got a lot more worries than that one," he told Fred.

Fred didn't seem to mind the laughter. "That's the one that bothers me most, though. That's all I ever really wanted to know about this whole mess. I didn't give a damn about the dumpin'—hell, I didn't even know about it till last night. If you really are gonna feed us to the gators here, I'd sure like to know who killed that other one."

"Why don't you ask your big-time investigator," Tolliver said. "It could be that he has it all figured out by now. After all, he's the one you paid."

"Ain't paid him yet," Fred said.

Tolliver laughed again. "Then you'll be saving yourself a little bit of money. How about it, Smith?"

"To hell with that shit," Merle said. "I think we oughta dump 'em in the lake and get outta here."

"We got time," Tolliver said. "Let's see what he knows."

My mouth was mostly clear of dirt, and I rolled onto my side so I could get a look at Tolliver. It wasn't easy to see him, since it was dark and I didn't want to twist my head up. All I could see were his boots and the bottoms of his pants.

"What I don't know," I said, "is how you're going to explain away the disappearance of four people, including one of your own deputies. I'd think that might be a little tricky."

"Just three people," Tolliver said. "Nobody's going to miss old Ransome, unless it's the people he worked for. And they won't say a single word. I think I can promise you that."

"But what about Jackson?"

"Oh, I suspect that word'll get around that he found out who was doing the rustling around here. Seems like it was old Fred Benton—can you believe that? That old fart's been around here all his life, and we all thought he was honest as the day is long. Fooled us all, that's for sure. But we all got suspicious when he brought in that city fella to work for him. Shows he wasn't to be trusted.

"But old Jackson got onto 'em some way or another, found out what they were up to with those cows. We got a call from him on the radio, and he'd chased 'em all the way into Fred's back forty. That's the last we ever heard of any of 'em. God knows what mighta happened to 'em back in those old lakes and marshes. They might all be dead, killed in a shoot-out. Gators probably ate ever' last bit of 'em."

He laughed. I was getting tired of hearing him do that. He really seemed to be having a good time, and I was tired of that, too. I just wished I could do something about it, which I couldn't.

"Hell," he said. "That story's close enough to the truth, after all. I imagine everyone around here will even believe most of it."

"If they search, they'll find the dump," I said, hoping to tone down the laughter.

"They will like hell," he said. "Who do you think'll be leading the search? And even if they do, none of the barrels are marked. Thanks to Jackson, we came back and got the one we screwed up on."

I had figured that. Jackson had obviously reported to Tolliver about Brenda's conversation with Perry. That accounted for the missing barrel.

"Who cares about that?" Merle said. "Let's shoot 'em and dump 'em."

"Damn right," Lonnie said. "I'm tired of listenin' to all this shit. They'd talk all night if it'd keep 'em out of the water."

"Hang on a minute," Tolliver said. "He still hasn't told us who killed Fred's gator."

"I don't know," I said.

"Damn," Fred said.

"Don't give up so easy," Tolliver said. "I bet he's got an idea or two, don't you, Smith?"

He was right. There was nothing I could prove, but I did think I knew the answer.

"Let's say it was Zach Holt. But he didn't do it on his own. You told him to."

"See there, Fred," Tolliver said. "You wouldn't have wasted your money on this fella even if you had paid him, not one bit. I knew he was a smart one, even before Jackson warned me. Didn't I, Jackson?"

His boots walked past my face, and he went over to Jackson and gave him a kick in the side. Jackson, who'd had very little to say until then, grunted when the boot hit him. Then he said, "I should've kept my mouth shut."

"Maybe so," Tolliver said. "But you told me he needed watching, and you were sure right."

He walked on back over to me. "Now tell 'em the rest," he said. His voice seemed to be coming from high above me.

"It was the rumors about the park that started it all, I think. You were afraid that if the land sold, the state would come in to build the park and maybe find all those barrels you thought were safely hidden. If that happened, Jackson might guess the truth about the rustling story, and you'd be in big trouble." I spit out a grass blade. "So you decided to scare Fred off."

"If that's what I decided, it sure as hell didn't work," Tolliver said.

I had been trying to hold my neck up and watch his legs, but it was too much work. I laid my head on the ground and went on.

"Oh, it worked all right. You didn't really want to scare him. Just the opposite. Fred told me himself that he was so stubborn that the more someone tried to make him leave, the more likely he was to stay. You knew what he was like, and so did everyone else. So you started in with the calls and the noises. And then you threw in the gator for good measure."

"That's pretty close, all right," Tolliver said. There was a note of something almost like admiration in his voice, as if he hadn't thought I'd really been able to figure things out.

"You got Holt to kill the gator and make the noises," I said. "And then I guess he got suspicious of why you wanted it done. Or maybe it was Ransome that paid him. Anyway, he caught on to what was happening and found out about the dumping. He even told someone about it."

That last bit wasn't true, but he'd hinted to Brenda Stone about what was going on, and I hoped the sheriff would worry just a little bit.

"I think that what happened next is that Holt got a tad greedy. He tried to blackmail you. Or Ransome. Whoever. One of you went over to his house to discuss things with him, got into an argument, and killed him. Since his wife was there, naturally she had to die too."

"Smart," Tolliver said. "Too damn smart for your own good, though."

"Yeah," Fred said. "I just wish he'd told me all this a little sooner. It mighta done some good."

"I put it together too late," I said.

"Not too late for us," Lonnie said. "Let's dump 'em."

"There's more," I said.

"Hell," Lonnie said. "I don't care."

"Let him tell it," Tolliver said, "it's better than *Columbo*."

"All right," I said. "When you and Ransome met to talk over Holt's murder, I followed Ransome part of the way to the meeting place. You tried to kill me then, since Jackson had already told you I was going to be trouble. I guess that's really about all. When I came in today with most of the pieces in place, after Jackson had already told you about what Fred and I had found down here, you knew it was time to take me out for good. Even if I did suspect the wrong man, you didn't want to take any chances with me. So you made that noise to get me and Fred down here, and we fell for it."

"And now here we all are together," Tolliver said, immensely pleased with himself.

"Who killed Holt?" Jackson said, lawman to the end. "You or Ransome?"

"Well, now," Tolliver said. "That's for me to know and you to find out. Sure gonna be hard for you to do, though, where you're gonna be."

"Now can we dump 'em?" Merle said.

"Sure," Tolliver said. "Let's dump 'em."

"We gonna shoot 'em first?" Merle said.

"Let the gators have 'em, the way they took Ransome," Tolliver said. "Alive and kicking, so they can appreciate the fun of it."

Someone grabbed my shoulders and began dragging me out into the water. They wouldn't have to shoot us. Put us in water over a foot or so deep, and we'd probably drown soon enough.

I heard splashing on either side of me. Fred and Jackson were being dragged into the lake as well. I tilted my head back to see who had me. It was Lonnie.

"I wish I could say you'll be sorry," I told him.

He didn't say anything, just kept dragging me.

When the water was about up to his waist, he let me go.

I thought that it might have been Ransome's thrashing around that got him in trouble, so I tried to hold still. I was working on the theory that if I didn't attract any attention, I'd be all right.

It was a good theory. The only thing wrong with it was the fact that I immediately sank to the bottom of the lake. It's not easy to stay calm in a situation like that.

Somehow I managed it. I got a deep breath before I went under, and I then lay there in the moss and weeds, feeling their rough tendrils on my face and trying to concentrate. The water had been only up to Lonnie's waist, hadn't it? Therefore, all I had to do was stand up, and then I could breathe.

Sounds easy, right? After all, I was in the water, which provided some buoyancy. It wasn't like lying on the ground.

So just try it sometime, with your hands and feet tied and thick, grasping water weeds all around you. It's not as easy as it sounds.

I was lying on my back, so the first thing I did was sit up. Even that wasn't easy, and I kept tangling in the weeds. I was beginning to think that I would attract an alligator before I got started, but I finally jackknifed myself into something resembling a seated position.

By then I needed to take a breath. I tried lunging upward, sort of like a merman, but I didn't accomplish a thing.

I sat for a second, thinking about it and telling myself not to panic. It shouldn't be so hard to move. After all, I was in the water, and the water would help me if I didn't try to fight it.

I tried bouncing up and down on my butt, each time straining my body upward and trying to get a little higher. It worked, and I managed at last to get my feet under me and force myself out of the water.

I came up covered with slimy moss, water draining out of my hair, vines hanging in front of my eyes. I sucked in a deep, gasping breath and then another, wondering how I could help Fred and Jackson.

Just about then, Jackson popped out of the water to my left, sucking air like a vacuum cleaner. He would be all right.

Then I saw the spotlight skittering across the surface of the water. It skittered right into me.

"He's mine," Tolliver said.

There was the crack of a rifle, probably Fred's. Or maybe it was the one Holt had shot at me with. Or neither of them. It didn't matter. I sank under the water, and Jackson went under at my side.

It seemed to me as if I were reliving another incident from my life, one in which I'd found myself involved in a similar situation. That time, though, I'd had a pistol in my hand, and I hadn't been trussed up like a hog-tied calf.

I came up again, saw the light, and ducked. Maybe it was only my imagination, but I thought I heard a bullet smack into the water right over my head.

I hadn't seen Jackson that time, and I still hadn't seen Fred. I wondered if he was still alive.

I came up again, shaking my head to clear the water from my eyes. The light was well off to my left, moving slowly. Either Jackson had just appeared or they were waiting for him.

I stayed low and hopped forward as quietly as I could, hoping to get a little closer to the shore. Nothing but my head was out of the water, which buoyed me up.

I looked over at the light and saw red eyes reflecting its beam. Jackson popped up right in front of it, and the men on the shore found him at once. He sank again, and the red eyes disappeared as well.

Those gators would get a bony meal if they went after Jackson, I thought. And where in the hell was Fred. Still at the bottom of the lake?

The light moved in my direction, and I slid under the water. This time when I came up, they might be waiting for me.

I stayed under for as long as I could, then eased my head out.

Someone nearly shot it off.

"I got 'im!" Merle yelled. Or something like that. It's hard to hear well when your ears are full of water and the pounding of your heart is sending out sound waves that could no doubt be detected on the other side of the lake.

I heard two more shots, but nothing hit the water over me. They were shooting at Jackson, or maybe Fred.

When my chest started hurting, I got ready to go up one more time. To hell with all this. I was going to hop as fast and as far as I could. If I got shot or if a gator grabbed me, fine. I was tired of being a target.

I was especially tired of being a part of Tolliver's private little shooting gallery.

I came up fast, not minding the noise or the splashing. The water was just about up to the tops of my thighs, and I hopped furiously forward.

Rifles and pistols started popping as I lunged along. I wasn't hit, but I fell face forward into the water.

That didn't stop me. I kept on kicking myself along as best I could with my bound legs.

There were more shots then, more than I would have expected unless Tolliver had more fire power than I thought.

I heard the distinctive sound of bullets hitting sheet metal, and the crashing of glass.

Had someone else joined the party?

Maybe so, and I started kicking, hopping, lunging—all at the same time. Anything to get out of the water, and to hell with the gators that might be closing in on me.

I couldn't get all the way out. When the water got too shallow, I could hardly make any progress at all, and finally I was slithering along like a crippled snake, trying to push myself through tangled weeds and slippery moss and sticky mud. I couldn't get out of the lake, but I made it so far that I could turn over on my back and lie there breathing with my nose out of the water.

I lay there and drank in the air and listened.

There was quite a bit of shooting, but no one yelled. It's hard to shoot accurately at the best of times, but in the dark, when you're excited, it's almost impossible except for the best of marksmen with the steeliest of nerves. So it was quite likely that no one had been hit.

I heard the truck start, a sound that was followed by a lot of hoarse cursing. Maybe Lonnie had been standing too far away to get in, and Tolliver was leaving him to fight it out on his own.

The motor revved, and I heard the spinning of the oversized tires as they fought for purchase in the soft ground. I could imagine the gobs of mud flying from under the tires.

The tires caught. I heard the truck buck forward.

There was a scream and a solid thump!, followed by another scream that was choked off abruptly.

Whoever was driving the truck—I strongly suspected Tolliver—had forcefully moved someone out of the way.

There was more shooting, and gradually the sound of the truck faded away. I lay there looking at the black sky, still heavily overcast, trying to get my breathing back to normal.

All the shooting stopped, and I could hear someone walking around in the grass. The normal night sounds—bugs, frogs, the water lapping around me—faded back in.

I decided that anybody who wanted to shoot Tolliver was almost certainly a friend of mine, so I called out. "Has anybody out there got a knife?"

"Papa's got one," Brenda Stone said. "Where are you?"

"Over here," I said.

I heard them walking in my direction.

$\triangledown$

19

As soon as they cut my hands and feet loose they started to look for Fred and Deputy Jackson. I would have helped, but I couldn't walk. I couldn't even stand up. I tried, but I felt as if my ankles and feet were missing.

I kicked my heels against the ground and slapped my hands together, trying to get the circulation started again. When I was successful, I wished I hadn't been. It felt almost exactly as I imagined it might feel if someone were trying to cut my hands and feet off with a fairly sharp knife. Then my fingers and toes began to burn and tingle, and it was as if they'd been stuck into a fire. I didn't scream, but I wanted to. Instead, I lay on the ground and moaned until the pain went away and I could stand up again.

They found Jackson sloshing around half-drowned and pulled him out of the water to cut the ropes. I didn't ever hear him yell, or even moan, but I liked to think that was because he hadn't been tied as tightly as I had.

Fred came out of it better off than any of us.

"Hell," he said later, "it was easy. Soon's I sunk down, I started to swim toward the shore. I got out before the shootin' even started, almost, but there wasn't a thing I could do to help you two, so I just stayed quiet. I figured it wouldn't do any good for me to yell out or anything. No use in all of us gettin' shot."

I asked him how he managed to swim, as trussed up as he was.

"Like a damn fish, that's how. They don't have any arms and legs, do they? I'm a little disappointed that you and Deppidy Jackson didn't figure that out for yourselves."

I just hoped that when I got as old as Fred—*if* I got to be that old—I'd be able to do half the things he could do. I don't know why I even bothered hoping, though, since I couldn't do half of them even at the age I was now.

The Stones, Brenda and her father-in-law, had come to our rescue unintentionally, armed with her .22 and his deer rifle. Brenda had heard the truck again and wondered what it had to do with our trip to the woods the previous night.

She was still certain that the dumping area had something to do with Holt's death, and of course she was right. I gathered that she didn't mention that fact to her father-in-law, however. She simply called him and told him that she'd heard the rustlers, that they were messing around in the woods below her house, that they might have killed Holt, and that if they were captured maybe Perry would go free. That was all the old man needed to hear. He grabbed up his deer rifle and drove to her house without a second thought.

"We got there just as they were throwing you-all in the back of that truck," Brenda said. "We didn't know who you were, but it sure didn't look right, them throwing you in the back all tied up like you were. We followed along to see what was going on, but we had to walk. I was afraid they might get so far ahead that we'd never find out what they were up to."

"Not me," Mr. Stone said. "I'd walk a hundred miles if it meant I could find out somethin' to get my boy out of that damn jail. You mean to tell me that the sheriff was in on that killin' all the time?"

We explained things as best we could. By then we were all crammed into the Jeep and on the way back to town. There hadn't been room for Ransome's body. We'd taken it out of the Jeep and left it behind to fend off the gators for itself.

"We saw all those barrels," Brenda said. "I wondered what they were."

I suspected they would still be there. I was pretty sure that Merle and Tolliver would have split up, with Merle taking the bobtail, but they wouldn't have taken the time to bury the barrels. That didn't matter any longer.

Lonnie hadn't gone with his pals. We'd left him right where Tolliver had left him, keeping Ransome company. Tolliver had finally managed to run somebody down with the truck. He'd smacked into Lonnie and run over his back with one of the tires, which had effectively ended Lonnie's career as a barrel handler, or as anything else.

We let Jackson out at the jail, where he was going to send out an APB on Tolliver and Merle. Brenda and Mr. Stone went in to tell Perry that he would almost certainly be getting out the next day, or as soon as Jackson could talk to a judge.

Fred and I took them home afterward, and then we took Jackson to pick up the county car he had used to drive to the dump site.

It had been an eventful evening.

Jackson came by Fred's house the next day. I was finally feeling dry again, and I'd almost decided that I'd take baths only once a week or so from now on. I hoped never to get into any body of water larger than a bathtub.

Jackson told us that Merle had been picked up by a sheriff's deputy on a farm-to-market road near Columbus and was telling everything he knew, which was enough to implicate Tolliver. We might never get Tolliver for the murders, but Jackson thought that we had a chance if he played things right. It meant test firing all Tolliver's personal weapons, including those recovered in a search of his house, but it was at least a possibility.

"We found a gator hide, too," Jackson said. "I went back and looked over Holt's property early this morning, and way down in the woods near the river he had a shack where he was curin' hides. There were two or three small ones, and one big one. That big one was yours, I guess, Fred."

"I don't want it," Fred said.

"Couldn't let you have it even if you did," Jackson said. "It's evidence."

I asked him if he thought Tolliver would be caught any-time soon.

"Sure he will. He won't be able to get very far in that truck. Too easy to recognize. Especially since old man Stone shot out one of the headlights and drilled the windshield a couple of times."

My own opinion was that by now some rice farmer was missing a pickup and had been given the county truck in its place. I thought that Tolliver was no doubt fording the Rio Grande by this time, but I didn't say so. It was up to Jackson and his law enforcement friends to find Tolliver now, not me. I'd solved the crime I'd come to investigate. I'd found out who killed the alligator.

"I hope that you get that rifle bullet from him one day and try matching it against Holt's rifles," I said. "Just to be sure."

"That's a mighty good idea," Fred said. "I'll remind you of it."

Jackson nodded, but he didn't make any promises.

After he left, Fred settled up with me, Mary fed me a substantial lunch, and I pointed the Subaru in the direction of Galveston.

The jacked-up truck came careening out of a side road and smashed into me less than a mile from Fred's house.

Tolliver hadn't left the county after all. He'd been waiting to get even.

I didn't see him coming. The road was at right angles to the one I was on, the truck hidden by the scrubby bushes growing along the fence row. I was listening to an oldies station and trying to reach the high notes along with Roy Orbison on "Only the Lonely."

I got a glimpse of something out of the corner of my eye, and then the truck clobbered me.

I was wearing my seat belt, which is the law in Texas, even if it did make me uncomfortable. So I stayed with the car as it rolled over and over.

I didn't try to count the rolls. My brain was spinning faster than the car. I was pretty sure that Tolliver had me this time.

He had hit me on the passenger side, which was the only good thing that happened.

He mashed my little Subaru like it was a bug.

The passenger door came over to meet me, and the seat folded up like a wet paper towel. The door on my side flew open, and if I hadn't been wearing the seat belt, I would have been about halfway to the Mexican border.

The Subaru either rolled through the ditch by the side of the road or it flew completely over it. I'll never know for sure, since there was no one there to videotape the incident for posterity.

The car went through a barbed-wire fence, and I think I remember hearing the strands of wire popping under the tension like a set of overwound guitar strings, but that may be simply a false memory. I was bouncing around so much that it shouldn't have been possible for me to hear anything like that.

Tolliver couldn't drive through the ditch to get me. He couldn't drive the truck across it. It was too deep and the sides were too steep, so he had to get out and come after me with his hands. Maybe he didn't have any more ammunition for the rifle.

By the time he'd gotten out of the truck, crossed the ditch, and come into the field where the car had finally stopped rolling, I had managed to unfasten the seat belt and get out of the car, which by some miracle had landed upright.

I was so disoriented that I was staggering around like a man who's just come off a four-day drunk. I was trying to walk, but I couldn't get my legs to work right. I wound up lurching around, trying to keep some distance between me and the car, which I was afraid would blow up at any moment.

It never did, possibly because there was hardly any gas in the tank. I'd been planning to drive by Hurley Eckles's store and fill it up on my way back to Galveston, at the same time filling Hurley up with the details of the gator story. It would have kept him and Temp amused for years.

As far as the Subaru was concerned, it might as well have blown up. It was a total loss either way.

There was no way I could defend myself from Tolliver. It was as if my brain had come loose from my skull. I was completely disoriented.

Tolliver, on the other hand, knew exactly what he wanted to do to me, which was to beat me to a pulp, and he proceeded to do it, yelling at the top of his lungs all the while.

I have no idea what he was yelling. He might have been incoherent, or it might have been that the words simply weren't registering on my brain as comprehensible sounds. The effect was the same.

He was hitting me right and left, and the blows weren't registering, any more than the words were.

I just didn't feel them.

That's not exactly right. I did feel them, but there was no pain. The message that I'd been hurt wasn't getting through. My brain had shut down the pain centers. I could feel Tolliver's fists thudding into my body, but that was all. There was contact, but no effect.

He started with a general pummeling, but when he saw that I wasn't hitting back, that I was more or less standing there staggering around like a human punching bag, he began to get more careful, aiming his punches, working first on my stomach, then my sternum, then my face.

It was a good solid right that finally woke me up. It jolted my head, split my lips, and sent shock waves all over my body. My brain was suddenly working again, and I immediately wished that it wasn't.

For the first time I realized that if I didn't put up some

kind of defense, Tolliver was going to kill me with his bare hands. In my brain-damaged shuffle, I hadn't even put up my own hands to protect myself.

Now I tried a few feeble blows that had little or no effect but did serve to turn aside Tolliver's fists. Waves of pain began to wash over me from his other blows and from the wreck.

The pain cleared my head. I saw Tolliver standing there, his hair awry, the white streak standing almost straight up, his eyes wild, his arms flailing as he came at me.

"SonuvabitchbastardI'llkillyoukillyou!" he screamed.

He obviously wasn't in a mood to be reasoned with or I might have asked him why he blamed me for his troubles. There were a lot of people who were more to blame than I was, not the least of whom was himself, but I had a feeling that he wouldn't see the point.

I tried to sidestep his charge, stumbled, and my bad knee gave way. It must have been hit in the crash.

Unable to slow his charge, Tolliver fell too, tripping over my feet.

We grappled on the muddy ground, and he worked himself on top of me, grasping my throat and squeezing, at the same time pounding my head into the ground and continuing his screaming.

"Sonuvabitchbastardkillyou!"

Nothing came out of my own mouth but a weak gasping noise as what breath I had left was being gradually choked off forever.

I went suddenly limp, then arched my back with all my strength, planting my heels and thrusting upward as hard as I could.

Tolliver pitched over my head, releasing his grip. I had been afraid he might hang on and rip my head off.

I made a quick roll, turning in time to see him flip himself over to face me again.

We were like two animals, crouched in the mud and grass, ready to tear each other's throats out.

He scuttled forward like some deformed land crab, moving

more quickly than I would have thought he could. If he got me this time, I was done for. My throat still felt as if his hands were wrapped around it, and my breath was short. My body ached all over. I could move only about a third as fast as he could. Maybe not even that fast.

He came straight at me, spreading his arms the better to gather me in and crush me.

I took a breath, lowered my head, and sprang at him, butting him in the face as hard as I could.

I heard the crunching of bones, felt his nose go soft, felt his teeth cave in.

I fell back, stunned. If he could get up now, he could have me. I didn't have anything left to face him with. I lay there on my back, my eyes open, staring at the sky, expecting to see him loom over me and raise his foot to smash my face the way I'd smashed his.

It didn't happen.

A few minutes passed, five or ten. I didn't count. I managed to push myself to a sitting position.

Tolliver lay a few feet away. At first I thought he might not be breathing, but then I saw the blood bubble in the area of his mangled nose.

The sight didn't particularly make me happy. He was a man who had committed murder, or had it done; a man who had raped the environment and possibly poisoned the land for years, or who had allowed it to happen; a man who had betrayed his office and the people who had elected him; and a man who had tried to frame others for his crimes.

If he had died, I wouldn't have wept for long.

As it was, he was alive, and I supposed it was my duty to get him to a hospital.

It took me quite a while to drag him back to the road. I had to rest a time or two. And it was almost impossible to heave him up into the cab of the truck. I finally got it done by propping him in the doorway, grabbing his legs, and heaving him up and in. He was more or less doubled up on the floor, but I didn't care.

He'd left the keys in the ignition. I started the truck and got out of there.

They kept me in the little hospital for a while, too, taking a few stitches here and there.

Then I had to take the truck back to the jail, to let Jackson know where his former boss was. Jackson gave me a ride back to the field, but the Subaru was a complete wreck. He told me that he'd have a wrecker sent for it. He thought that the driver might buy it to pay for the hauling fee.

All in all, it was a long day.

When I got back to Galveston, it was late afternoon. Dino was at the house, feeding Nameless, or trying to. Nameless was nowhere to be seen. Dino was standing on the porch, looking suspiciously like a man calling "Here, kitty, kitty, kitty," with his hand up to his mouth, but he stopped calling and put his hand down when he saw me coming.

He relaxed when he recognized me. "Where in hell did you get that thing?" he said. "You look like an extra in an old John Wayne movie."

"I take it that you're referring to this genuine World War Two Jeep," I said, stopping and getting out.

"Yeah, the Jeep," he said. "I don't think I've seen one like that lately. The kind they make now, all the kids drive 'em, and they look like yuppie cars."

"Well, this is the real thing. I guess you might say it was part of my fee."

He gave me the once over. "Sure looks like you earned it. You crack the case?"

I was about to answer when Nameless meandered nonchalantly around the corner of the bushes that surrounded the house. He gave me a casual glance, then walked over to his food bowl.

"It must be nice to be loved," Dino said.

"He has difficulty expressing joy," I said.

"Sure he does. Anyway, how about it? You put the Sherlock Holmes on those mainlanders?"

"I don't think I'd put it that way, exactly. But I did what I was hired to do."

"What was that, anyway? You never did say."

I thought about it for a minute, watching Nameless gobble the Tender Vittles. "I found out who killed the alligator," I said. "Let's go in and have a Big Red."

Dino simulated gagging. He wasn't fond of Big Red.

"I gotta go," he said. "I watch *Miami Vice* every night on cable, the USA channel. Tell me about that alligator sometime, though, huh?"

I thought about Crockett and Tubbs.

I thought about Tolliver banging my head against the ground with his hands locked around my throat.

"Sure, I said. "Sometime."